Simon Williams

The Light From Far Below

Also by the same author, for children and teens:

Summer's Dark Waters

For adults:

Oblivion's Forge
Secret Roads
The Endless Shore
The Spiral Heart
Salvation's Door

For K.

"You're the light from another world"

"Joe. Wake up. Wake up!"

His eyes blinked open. Emma looked down at him from the gloom, a backpack slung over her shoulder. "What's going on?" he whispered as he sat up.

Emma sat on the side of his bed. She didn't say anything at first, and Joe felt a chill stir inside him. He was about to ask her again when she suddenly spoke. "Something that we've feared for a while. We didn't want to tell you or Amber until we had to."

Joe stared at her. His mouth suddenly felt bone dry. "Tell me *what?*"

"The Order... they're not what we thought. They haven't been for a long while, as far as we can tell."

Joe struggled to understand. His remaining sleepiness fell away, replaced by a sense of crawling horror. "I don't... what do you..."

"To put it simply, the leaders of the Order have been working with those of the Lost. They're simply two faces of the same coin, Joe. The same thing, more or less. And we found out that they have plans for us. Not the sort we want to be involved in."

Joe looked in bewilderment at her backpack. "Is that why we're going? I mean, do we have to go right now? It's the middle of the night!"

"Yes, we do." She got up. "You've got ten minutes to get dressed and get your things together. Put some clothes and whatever else will fit into your backpack. That's all you can take with you."

Joe looked aghast at her. "I'm sorry," she whispered. "I wish things could be different. But they're not."

She left the room and Joe was alone again in a whirlwind of silence.

He packed in silence, numb inside. When he made his way downstairs and took his coat from the peg in the hallway he saw Emma pacing around in the living-room through the open door. She noticed him and came through. "You need to give me your phone," she said.

"What? No way! I haven't used it for anything I shouldn't..."

"Joe, we need to make it as difficult as possible for them to track us. I don't have time to argue with you. *Give me the phone.*"

Helplessly he pulled the phone out of his pocket and gave it to Emma. She held it in her left palm and pressed her right hand on top of the screen, then closed her eyes. Joe watched as thin tendrils of smoke drifted upwards from the phone.

"You didn't have to do that," he muttered resentfully as she lifted her hand and opened her eyes. The phone crumbled into black dust as she squeezed it. "What about yours?" he asked.

"I thought you might say that." Emma took her phone out of her jeans pocket and destroyed it in the same way. Even in his state of confusion it occurred to Joe that had anyone else seen his aunt use her powers like this they would have questioned their own sanity. It should have been impossible. But so many impossible things in his life had happened anyway.

Joe watched speechlessly as Emma wiped the ashen remains of the phone from her hands. "I'm sorry we have to do this," she said quietly. "But we have no choice."

He followed her outside. The night was humid and sticky even for July. Emma unlocked the car and got into the driver's seat. Joe opened the door and sat in the front passenger seat. "What about Amber and Luke?" he asked suddenly.

"Close the door," Emma told him. When he did, she started the car and began to drive down the road. "What about *Amber and Luke?*" Joe asked again, more urgently. "Their house is *that* way," he added when Emma drove past the next road junction.

Suddenly he saw that Emma was crying. "What is it? What's wrong?" he demanded, terrified without knowing why.

"We're going our way... and they're going theirs," his aunt managed to say eventually. "That's just the way it is."

"But we..." Joe tried to swallow down his panic. "We haven't had a chance to say goodbye! Can't we just..."

Emma just shook her head. Tears streamed down her face as she kept her eyes on the road ahead. Aghast and lost for words, Joe looked away and into the night.

AMBER

1

Restless and consumed by gloomy thoughts, Amber paced slowly around her bedroom and finally wandered over to the window. The usually drab grey apartment blocks that filled her view were suddenly transformed as the red blush of the day's last sunlight painted itself onto their surfaces. Every time she saw a sunset here, which wasn't often during this damp early winter of low, dark cloud, its beauty startled her. For a short while the awful monotone of the grey city landscape looked alive with fire.

It's still a waste of a sunset, Amber thought morosely as she tapped her fingers on the windowsill. A minute or two later the sun disappeared over the jagged skyline of distant buildings, and as the light faded she sighed and went to sit on the edge of her bed. She stared at the clothes she had placed there earlier for no other reason than to remind herself of how few items of clothing she had these days- three pairs of socks and pants, three t-shirts, three bras, a pair of jeans, two tops and two hoodies.

Next to her clothes lay a couple of tatty old books, both with their corners curled up and at least a few pages missing, and a notebook that she had used on and off as a diary for the last year and a third, ever since she and Joe had been parted. Amber hadn't finished reading either book and had finally abandoned the diary weeks ago. She had opened it occasionally since then to read the last few entries but couldn't think of anything more to write. What was the point? It didn't help her situation. Anyway, who would ever read it apart from her? Sometimes she felt embarrassed and almost angry at the things she'd written, especially if she had been emotional at the time. They never seemed to make as much sense in the days or weeks afterwards. Some felt ridiculous when she read them again.

This is all I have left in my life, she thought. *It fits in a backpack.*

Amber didn't cry often anymore, determined to keep her emotions on the inside in an effort to manage them and at least *try* to present a normal face to the world, despite the fact that her life had been out of control for so long. But emotions always threatened to spill out, and the worst of them was the constant fear. People working for the Order could be anywhere and look like anyone, so Amber had decided to assume that their enemies were *everywhere* at once and that no one could be trusted. That helped her feel a bit safer, or at least a bit more prepared. Not much, but a little.

In any case she had no one to trust except her dad these days. She had no friends, spoke to no one unless she had to, and certainly didn't have any social media accounts. Some days she wondered if any students at her old school still talked about her or even asked one another where she might be. *Probably not,* she always told herself, *and that's for the best. To not be remembered and leave no trail.* Her dad had spoken about "erasing digital footprints" a lot since they'd left their home. Whatever he had done, Amber just hoped that he'd done it thoroughly.

Amber couldn't remember much detail from that hot, humid night the summer before last when they had left their home. She recalled being oddly detached from everything at one point. The street lights blurred and smeared across her vision like a bad photograph. She remembered the taste of tears, and her throat hurting from screaming at her dad as they drove away into the night.

Those hours had been some of the worst in Amber's entire life. Mostly she could only recall the way she had felt when her dad had revealed that they weren't going to see Joe and Emma again. She had cried and shouted and raged and no doubt said all sorts of horrible things to her dad. The sounds she had made had frightened her, as if the tortuous experience had put her only one step away from turning into some terrible, inhuman creature. *What must I have looked like?* she had wondered for days afterwards.

Oddly, she remembered the expression on his face with perfect clarity. He had been outwardly calm, but the anger in his eyes had finally made her fury ebb away. *I know what you feel,* they had told her without his needing to speak. *Because I feel it too.*

They had changed vehicles sometime in the small hours- she still had no idea how her dad had organised that- and had then driven until dawn, after which her dad parked the car in the lay-by of a country lane. They walked for a while before they reached a town, where they stayed for a few days. From that point on it had been a matter of staying somewhere for a short while before they eventually had to move on. Her dad eventually sorted out IDs for them, and even arranged for her to attend school from time to time, but it had never been for very long. Amber was just astonished that the various authorities accepted her identification.

In the days leading up to their departure, her dad had acted in a way that Amber might once have called paranoid until she realised how the world really worked. Joe had told her that Emma had been much the same. "They're up to something," he had said worriedly.

When she thought back to that time, Amber remembered the darkness that had fallen over them both while they should have been enjoying the summer holidays and trying to put what they remembered of their recent experiences behind them. *Maybe we knew deep down that we wouldn't be together for much longer,* she thought. *We just tried to pretend otherwise. We tried to ignore the shadow.*

Amber picked up one of the books from her bed and thought suddenly that the sorry-looking volume was a bit like her. She had pages missing from her story too. The finer detail of her journey through the Emptiness remained frustratingly vague. *In time, you'll remember everything you thought you'd forgotten,* her dad had told her, but Amber wasn't satisfied. What did "in time" mean, anyway? She didn't want to recall every last detail, but not being able to remember those events clearly felt even worse.

Occasionally she thought she might be able to remember names or faces, but the idea faded quickly away like the remains of a dream in the morning.

Amber suspected that her dad had done something to make her memory of the Emptiness fade more than it should have done. She had asked him at least a dozen times to help her remember. But each time he had said, "I'm sorry but it isn't that simple. It will come back when you're ready. That's just the way it works."

Amber was not a naturally patient girl. The idea of *waiting* to be ready was maddening, especially as neither she nor her dad could say how long the wait might be.

The worst thing about their lives wasn't even that they had to move around from place to place frequently, although that was bad enough. Being separated from Joe but still able to vaguely sense him out there felt like a kind of torture. The feeling ebbed and flowed. Sometimes it felt like nothing stronger than belief, but on other occasions it was as if she could sense how he was feeling. When that happened, worry and sadness washed through her. They were *his* emotions as well, Amber knew. Somehow they reached her, even though it couldn't be possible. How could feelings travel from place to place?

But I've seen the impossible, she would remind herself. *I just don't remember much about it.*

Joe was therefore everywhere and nowhere at the same time. She couldn't tell which direction he was in or how far away he might be. One time, out of sheer frustration she had tried to describe the sensation to her dad. He had said, "This might sound awful, but it's just as well you can't tell where he is. I can't be sure that you wouldn't leave to try and find him."

Amber had stared indignantly at him. "I promised I wouldn't!"

"You know it was too dangerous for the four of us to be together," he had warned. "I explained why."

"You don't trust me," she had said resentfully.

"Not where this is concerned. Tell me honestly- do you trust yourself?" he had replied, and Amber hadn't answered. She couldn't truthfully say that she definitely *wouldn't* sneak away and try to find Joe, even though it would have been impossible, not to mention incredibly dangerous.

Either she or her dad- or usually both of them- would know when one or more of their enemies appeared somewhere in the neighbourhood. A kind of sixth sense alerted her when they were nearby. Her dad had pointed out it didn't mean that these individuals were hunting them. The Order had many plans. Amber reckoned there wasn't any town in the country or even the entire world where they didn't have at least several people engaged in one plot or another. The chaos ran deep and wide.

"How many are there in the Order?" she had asked her dad one time.

"Many thousands," he had told her. "Are you surprised?"

"I'm surprised they can all keep the truth a secret, I guess," Amber had admitted after a moment.

"Very few of them know the truth, Amber. That's the trick. Some of them don't even *know* who and what they're working for. Most just do as they're told, for reasons that might not even have anything to do with the Order, at least directly. Hurt a few people here and there, make a few threats, put up some posts on the Internet, deliver a package... it's the final effect that matters. They're just tiny cogs in the machine."

Amber hadn't been quite sure what he meant by that, but his words had disturbed her. They implied that people were like blind insects driven by nothing more than idle selfishness, with one goal programmed deeply into them. The destruction of their own race.

"Sooner or later they're all going to start pulling in the same direction," her dad had said one time, "and when they do the world is going to be in deep trouble. The dominos will fall."

She hated having to go outside, into a city that teemed with people. Sometimes even the thought would make her stomach tighten with fear. This was a horrible part of the city, full of tension and the sense that a riot might happen at any time, Amber had thought more than once as she hurried back from the shops with her dad and tried to avoid the mean and hungry stares of the groups of boys (and sometimes girls) they had to walk past. *We've done nothing wrong, but we're always the ones who have to look away and try to avoid confrontations,* she often reasoned. *Why is the world so full of hate and violence? Sometimes I can even feel it inside myself, simmering away like it's about to erupt. Does it infect everyone sooner or later, a sort of directionless rage? Where does something like that come from, so powerful that it reaches into everyone and changes them?*

15

"We've evolved as far as we're going to evolve and now we're going quickly backwards," her dad had said one time as they quietly discussed life, society and their own furtive existence. "Nobody's interested in anything unless it involves a quick fix or a cheap thrill for themselves. Doing things for others isn't even on most people's radars anymore."

Amber reckoned he was right. She didn't need him to tell her. She could see it in everyone's eyes.

Only last week as they walked through a nearby park with some food shopping- that was usually the only reason they went out- Amber had felt that uncomfortable, prickly and nauseous sensation which had grown horribly familiar to her recently. It meant that people of the Order were nearby.

She had looked around and immediately noticed a group of boys gathered at a bench drinking and smoking. *It's them!* shouted a panicked voice in her head. She had started to walk more quickly to get past them, especially when one of the boys fixed her with a feral, malevolent stare. But her dad had caught her arm gently and said in a quiet voice, "It's not them."

Amber had looked carefully around until she saw two men and a woman gathered together on the other side of the park fountain they had just walked past. They were dressed in grey suits and held umbrellas and briefcases. All three looked as if they'd just come out of a boring business meeting or conference. *There they are,* she realised suddenly. For a moment she thought she could see faint lines and symbols move on their heads, but otherwise they looked entirely ordinary.

Neither Amber nor her dad had said anything after that until they arrived back at the poky little apartment where they had lived for the last month. But almost as soon as they got back they had argued.

Maybe seeing three of their enemies so near had caused her to stress out even more than usual. "I can't bear this place!" she had shouted at one point. "Do you have *any* idea what it's like?"

"Why don't you tell me?" he had suggested. His quiet words made her feel embarrassed, as if she was just an angry kid who couldn't control her mood from one moment to the next. "Tell me what it's like."

He had sounded sarcastic, which he often did when *he* was upset. And she knew that *he* was angry as well, even though he hadn't raised his voice.

Amber had taken a deep breath and tried to collect her thoughts. "When I wake up every morning, just for a second it's as if I've forgotten about everything that's happened. And then I suddenly remember how things are, and it feels like a stone has fallen through me. I remember who I am and *where* I am. I remember that we're not where we lived for years, and that everything is messed up and we just keep moving. I just want to go back to sleep and make this world disappear. Our enemies are everywhere and it doesn't matter where we go. We can't ever rest. It never stops..."   ,

Amber remembered that she had almost started to cry at that point but somehow managed to carry on, although her voice shook as she tried to speak. "...and I can't... I can't go and see Joe now that he's not just down the road. I miss him so much, Dad. I feel a heavy weight inside me every time I think of him, and it's the same *every single day*. Can you imagine that?"

"I can," he had said quietly. "I'm sorry, Amber. You know I didn't want the four of us to be separated, but it was safer this way."

"Was it? I don't *feel* safe. We both know that our enemies are somewhere nearby every time we go out. The Order are never far away. How can there be so *many* of them?"

"Something big is happening. There are more now than ever before. Their net has spread further and faster than I thought..."

"Net? You mean the dark net, online?"

"Not just that. I haven't been able to find out what it is. It's hard to get enough information without putting us in more danger."

"If we were all still together..."

"...then it would be easier for them to find us." He had sighed and sat down wearily, head in hands. "Amber, we've been through this so many times, and doing it again isn't going to change anything."

"Joe and I are meant to be *together!*"

Amber cringed as she recalled what she had said, and the fact that she hadn't even bothered to wait for his reply. She had just turned and ran to her bedroom and slammed the door shut as if she was still a little girl throwing a hissy fit.

She sighed. *I can't believe I said that. Joe and I are meant to be together? What must that have sounded like?! He was my best friend but I made him sound like he was a boyfriend or something! How is Dad ever going to take me seriously if I keep doing things like that?*

19

Amber glanced at the bedroom window again as cold wintry rain began to lash against it. The good weather had lasted about ten minutes.

Restless and frustrated, she wandered back over to the window and stared morosely out into the gloom. At times like this she liked to let that grey bleakness to sink into her distracted thoughts. Somehow it made the fear fade away a little.

The high-rise block of flats opposite looked even worse than the one where they lived. Chunks of plaster had come away from the wall in many places, almost as if the building belonged in a war zone. The window fittings were rotten and had started to disintegrate. Scrawls of ancient graffiti, none of which made any sense to her, covered large parts of the damp, cracked surface- tags drawn by people who were now probably the same age as her dad. Amber saw a woman stare blankly out of her kitchen window as she dried her dishes. She had paused the chore for a moment, as if she'd forgotten what she was doing or no longer saw any point in doing it. A plate was clutched in both hands almost like a joke trophy. *Look what I've won,* the woman's pose seemed to say. *A lifetime spent here, walking from room to room, doing the chores and watching daytime television until my body gives up.*

Amber found the scene unsettling. She shuddered and looked elsewhere and saw an office worker standing by one of the windows in another block, which was rented out to various companies. He held some papers and stared out into the coming night as if lost in deep thought. Perhaps he was counting down the minutes until he could go home. Amber couldn't make out his expression from where she stood, but she imagined that he looked desperately sad, as if he needed to find himself a different existence, a door that led somewhere better.

That's what I need to do, she thought. *Step away from it all. Because this isn't any sort of life at all. It has to change, but it won't unless we're eventually caught, and that would be even worse.*

The rain soon smudged her view of the urban hell. Amber turned away and lay down on her bed, then closed her eyes. She had never been able to sleep this early in the day but needed to shut the world out for a little while.

Perhaps she *did* drift off to sleep somehow, because when Amber opened her eyes later her room was dark. The rain still came down outside, heavier than before. She sat up and was about to go and close the curtains and switch her bedside lamp on when she heard Joe's voice.

"Amber?"

She almost jumped out of her skin. A strange sensation crept over her skin like a wave. "Joe!" she gasped, and fumbled for the switch of her lamp, almost knocking it over in her haste.

She switched her lamp on and light filled the room.

Her empty room.

You imagined it, she told herself bitterly in the aftermath as her heart pounded. *It wasn't the first time you thought you heard his voice, and it probably won't be the last.*

But this time it felt different. The sound of his voice had been so *real* that just for a moment Amber had been convinced that Joe was in the room with her. *It wasn't inside my head,* she told herself. *It wasn't!*

Amber sat on the edge of the bed and took several deep breaths to try and calm herself. *I'm going mad,* she reasoned. *I miss him so much, of course I want to think it was real even if it can't have been.*

But the Emptiness was both impossible *and* real. Why couldn't this be?

Finally she plucked up the courage to speak his name, but when she heard herself say the word it sounded silly- just an empty, pointless word. *Of course he's not here,* she thought scornfully. *Can you see him?*

Amber was suddenly reminded of how it had all started, almost a year and a half ago. Joe had claimed he heard a voice in his head, and her instinct had been to doubt him. She had instead worried about his mental health and feared that one way or another she would lose her best friend to a darkness inside his own head.

But the truth had turned out to be far stranger than they could have imagined.

Something hard suddenly hit the window. Amber jumped and turned to see a web of cracks spread from a whitened area of the glass which must have been hit by a stone. Windows were often smashed in their block, but no one had broken one of theirs before. Usually the vandals would choose easier targets on the ground floor.

I'd better go and tell Dad, she thought nervously, and got up. But then, as she stared at the window the same sound occurred again and another impact pattern spread from a different part of the glass. But she didn't see anything strike the surface. It was as if *invisible* stones were hitting the glass.

Amber ran to the door, flung it open and shouted "Dad!" only to find that he was already just outside the door. She was about to tell him what had happened but he motioned for her to follow him. She saw a hard, determined look in his eyes and her heart lurched. "Have they... have they found us?" she stammered.

"I'm sorry, Amber," he said as he turned to face her. "I made a mistake. It was bound to happen sooner or later." He hugged her impulsively. "I love you," he whispered in her ear. "Remember what I told you. Always remember."

His words seemed so final that they terrified her. "No!" she cried and grabbed at him. "No, it can't be like this! Don't go! You can't go!"

But before he could reply they heard a loud knocking on their apartment door- one, a short silence, then two, another short silence, and finally three.

"Which way will it be?" came a voice from outside in the grim corridor. Unbelievably, it actually *sang* the words. Amber felt her skin crawl. It sounded like the voice of an overweight old man, a breathless message that crept through the space under their door and into their apartment, somehow made louder so they could hear it perfectly. "The easy way... or the hard way?" it continued, and the stark choice it offered was followed by a harsh cackle that almost lost itself in a choking fit.

Suddenly a different voice spoke. This one was female, clear, impatient and probably owned by someone much younger. "Luke? Amber? We know you're in there. We wouldn't have wasted our time coming here if we didn't know. You've got a decision to make. Let us in and we can talk about how you can start making up for your... wayward behaviour. Your other choice is that you continue to ignore us, and then we'll have to force our way in and tear you to pieces. It really is that simple. No tricks, just promises. You have twenty seconds."

Amber had never felt so scared in her life. They *have human voices, but they're not people, they're monsters in the skins of people,* she thought in terror. There could be no escape this time. This was the end, and it was all going to happen far more quickly than she could have expected.

"This is what we're going to do..." her dad whispered, but before he could say anything else the apartment door split open and everything descended into chaos.

The shapes that came towards them moved with unbelievable speed. Amber screamed, and the sound seemed to come not only from inside her but from everywhere around. She held up her hands as if to defend herself and wondered bleakly how long it would take them to destroy her.

And then she felt something both alien and familiar wake inside her, a force that had broken free at last. Her vision became brighter and their enemies darkened. Time slowed down, or at least everyone appeared to move more slowly. The sounds around her became a continuous dull roar.

A jagged black arm or tendril cut savagely through the illumination and reached for her. But then it recoiled as if something had burned it. *They can't touch me,* a voice spoke up in Amber's head. *They can't touch me, but I can destroy them.*

But she saw that some of the creatures had already surrounded her dad. Desperately she tried to step towards him, but now she had slowed down as well. The steady, droning wall of sound continued. For a moment Amber caught sight of a young woman with a thin body and gaunt face. She wore a long leather coat that hung over her body like a shroud. *I know you!* Amber thought suddenly, but she had no idea where from.

Her dad fought furiously against the dark creatures. They changed shape every moment so that even with time slowed down they appeared as little more than a blur. Every time he threw them back they resumed their attacks on him, relentless and more ferocious than ever.

I'll kill them all! came a shriek inside her, and Amber tried again to move towards their enemies. They had given up on her now and instead surrounded her dad, a writhing blanket of darkness. Sooner or later he would be too weak to resist and then it would all be over.

"No!" Amber screamed, but as she redoubled her attempts to destroy the invaders, the brightness all around her become unbearable, and her sight of her surroundings slowly vanished out of view.

The light was the last thing she saw before her vision faded completely and she fell forward, no longer aware of anything.

2

Amber woke up suddenly. She lay on the floor of the living room. Every part of her ached as if she had been beaten up. She groaned in pain and sat up, shivering. The curtains were still drawn. Somewhere outside she could hear a faint but steady thumping rhythm as if someone in one of the neighbouring blocks was playing dance music.

She put her hands to her head and tried to remember what had happened, but all she could recall was a muddled image of light and shadow and a woman who looked directly at her with a faint smile of triumph on her lips.

As she glanced down at her shaking hands, Amber caught sight of several black lines under her skin that she hadn't seen before, like dark veins. *Oh my god,* she thought fearfully. *What are those?* But even as she stared at them and wondered what had happened to her the marks faded out of view and left no visible trace.

They came for us, she remembered suddenly. *They forced their way in and I fought back and they couldn't touch me. Then it all went white as if light poured over everything...*

"Dad?" she called out. Her voice trembled noticeably. No answer came, so she called again and when she still heard nothing, Amber got to her feet and looked in every room in their apartment. *Please be somewhere in here,* she thought each time she paused outside the door of each room before opening it. *Maybe he's ok, just asleep like I was. He must be somewhere here. He wouldn't have just woken up and left without me.*

But she didn't find her father anywhere.

All sorts of thoughts rushed through her head. *They took him. They overpowered him and they must have taken him away. Did they...*

Did they kill him?

Amber's eyes filled with desperate tears. Finally she sat on the sofa with her head in her hands. She couldn't bear the violent images that raced through her head, each one worse than the last. She tried not to imagine what they might have done to him, but it was impossible not to. "No!" she moaned to herself.

After a while Amber remembered something her dad had said to her a number of times over the last year or so- something she hadn't wanted to listen to. *I won't always be able to protect you,* he had said. *I'll do my best, but you need to realise I won't be around forever. One day they could come for us, and we don't know what will happen that day. We can only try to be ready.*

And they had tried. They had prepared as much as they could without risking unwanted attention. Amber had been trained in the basics of self-defence, judo and karate. Her dad had even showed her how to fight with a knife. *I hope you'll never have to use these skills,* he had once told her before adding sadly, *But you will. That's the way of the world.*

What did I do to stop them? Amber wondered frantically. *Something happened inside me. Something woke up. And where did that light come from? Was it something that Dad did, a final effort to protect me from our enemies?*

Or something that we both did at the same time?

She had known she was different to other people ever since her dad and Emma told her and Joe the truth about them all, and she had *felt* different ever since her time in the Emptiness. But she knew that this was much more powerful- something wild, dangerous, uncontrollable.

Not human, Amber thought as she remembered the black marks that had appeared for a moment, then told herself not to be so stupid. *Don't think crazy thoughts like that!*

She took a deep breath and wiped tears from her eyes. Then she noticed something so odd that she began to question her own sanity.

Their apartment door, which the people from the Order had broken through, now looked completely undamaged.

That's impossible, Amber thought as she walked to the door and stared at it in disbelief. Not even the slightest scratch could be seen on its surface- at least, none that hadn't already been there when the two of them moved in a month ago.

Trapped in a nightmare that she couldn't understand, Amber took a deep breath and turned the handle.

As soon as Amber closed the door behind her and stood in the dismal grey corridor, the faint sounds of music stopped. For a moment she panicked, fearful that she had left her door key in their apartment. Then she found it in her pocket and sighed in relief.

All she could hear, apart from the thump of her heart, was the sound of water as it dripped from the leaky ceiling, one of many problems that the maintenance company had still failed to fix. It sounded louder than ever now, almost as if it might be the only sound in the world.

Amber listened intently for a while but heard nothing at all from the neighbouring flats, which was unusual. The couple who lived next to them on one side spent their days and evenings fighting or arguing, but today no sounds at all came from their apartment. The man who lived directly across the corridor played loud music almost all the time, but right now he wasn't.

The silence all around unsettled her so much that Amber considered knocking on the door of the man opposite, or even the psycho couple in the apartment next to theirs. She just wanted to hear human voices, even angry ones. But then she imagined herself asking her neighbours, *Did you hear a disturbance? Did you see anything out of the ordinary?* Or even *Have you seen my dad anywhere?* That would be the worst question of all to ask, revealing that she was alone.

Anyway, no one around here answered their doors unless they had to.

"Did it even happen?" she whispered. "Am I dreaming?" Even the faint sound of her voice sounded strangely loud and harsh in the suffocating silence of the corridor. "The door is different," she told herself as she looked at it again.

A far more unpleasant question occurred to her, and it raised a troubling possibility. Was she going mad?

Amber realised suddenly that the door opposite stood very slightly open. *How did I not notice that before?* she wondered. She plucked up the courage to walk a little further down the corridor and stared in open-mouthed shock as she saw that the next doors on both sides were also slightly open. Amber ran quickly back to her own door and pulled the key from her pocket. Her hands trembled violently and she dropped her key twice before she managed to open the door.

She stepped hurriedly back into their apartment. But no sooner had she slammed the door behind her than she realised that something else had changed.

All the rooms in their apartment, she discovered as she wandered from each one to the next, were now empty except for the carpet and curtains. She could find none of their belongings or even the furniture anywhere. The entire place looked as bare as if it was still being offered for rent, except without even the furniture. It contained no evidence that she and her dad had ever lived here.

But it wasn't like this when I woke up just a short while ago, she thought desperately. *Or was it? Did I just not notice? How could I not have noticed? It's like everything I know is being erased!*

Amber felt too numb to do anything except forcefully tell herself that she had become caught in a powerful dream. *I will wake,* she decided. *I just have to get through this.*

Helplessly she went out into the corridor again. The drip of the water from the ceiling sounded louder than ever and even faster now, as if the volume and the tempo were a message that she'd started to run out of time.

Amber summoned up the courage to push the doors of each neighbouring apartment wide open, and each time she saw nothing but emptiness in the hallways and rooms beyond, as if everyone had moved out suddenly and at the same time.

Emptiness, she thought again, and the word stuck in her mind until the full horror of the situation dawned on her.

The Emptiness!

Consumed by panic, Amber ran headlong down the corridor. She didn't bother to shut the door to their apartment behind her. What was left in there anyway? She half-ran, half-leapt down the stairs towards the ground level. Even though she was wearing soft-soled trainers the sounds they made echoed harshly around the deserted building. She tripped on one of the steps and fell down several more. She got shakily to her feet and gave her grazed palms only a quick look then continued down each flight of stairs, a little more carefully but still as quickly as she dared.

Finally Amber reached the door that led outside into the grounds of the apartment block and from there the street beyond.

"Be calm," she said quietly. "Just be calm. You're dreaming. Be calm." But that just reminded her

31

of her old KEEP CALM, IT'S JUST THE END OF THE WORLD T-shirt, which had now vanished along with everything else.

It's just the end of the world. The words echoed desolately around in her head.

Amber pulled the handle, opened the door and stepped outside, and the Emptiness opened up before her.

3

So many stars lit up the sky that the scene took her breath away.

Everywhere Amber looked, points of light dotted the heavens. Some of them were as bright as Venus. Many glittered with a pure white brilliance while others had a slightly blue, red or even green glow. Their combined power made the night as bright as one with a full moon, although the moon was nowhere to be seen.

Amber was so astonished that she forgot everything else for a short while and simply stood and gazed at the sheer beauty of the night sky. After a moment she recalled a night years ago- she had been seven at the time- when she had gone for a walk in the countryside with her dad late in the evening. She remembered how intensely cold that night had been, with frost already forming on the ground. For some reason she had felt so alert, so full of energy, so *alive* that night. She had skipped and jumped more than walked and had several of giggling fits for no reason other than that she had felt insanely happy, without a care in the world.

A forest of stars had mapped out the sky that night. Far fewer than this alien display, but she remembered that she'd felt almost the same way when she stared up at them.

That had been the night when her dad had shown her the visible planets for the first time, and the constellations like Orion and the Plough. *None of them are here,* she thought. *There's nothing I recognise. This might not even be the same universe.*

That incomprehensible idea pulled her suddenly back into her dire situation. "Dad," she whispered, but he wasn't here. *You miss him now it's too late,* she told herself. *Now you're alone and you have no one.*

"Shut up," Amber told herself, as loudly as she dared. With an effort she crushed her thoughts of what might have happened to him and walked as far as the silent and deserted street.

As she looked up at the darkened windows in the empty apartment blocks and other buildings nearby, Amber felt goose bumps prickle her skin all over. She felt certain that something approached, or perhaps looked out from all the windows at the same time. *Hide!* she thought frantically, and suddenly felt certain that she knew where her enemy approached from.

She set off at a brisk walk in the opposite direction. Every few seconds she stopped and looked back, but nothing made itself known and the only sound Amber heard was her own soft footfall. One of the streetlights still worked, but it flickered as if it might be faulty or about to fail completely.

Amber stopped for a little longer at one point to see if she could still detect the creature nearby, but she couldn't. Her breath drifted up into the chilly air as she listened to the pounding of her heart.

She recalled the moments just after she and Joe had reached the Emptiness before. The cottage where they had been just before and after they found their way into the Emptiness had looked almost the same from the inside but less so from the outside, and the further they walked away from it the less the whole area resembled the world they knew. They hadn't stepped into the Emptiness so much as drifted into it.

Maybe the way it looked depended on where you got to it from.

"I don't know what to do," Amber whispered, and panic threatened to overcome her completely. The street lamp that was still lit made a sudden buzzing sound and Amber jumped and looked as it flickered desperately a few times and went out. Immediately the street darkened and the alien stars appeared even brighter than before as if to make up for the gloom.

The street lamps don't belong here, Amber thought. *Things that don't belong here will stop working sooner or later. Things from the world I know are brought here with me but then they fade away.*

Amber continued along the road. Here and there she saw what looked like litter on the pavement, although the closer she peered at it the less distinct it appeared, as if the letters and branding became blurred when she tried to inspect them. When she looked closer still, she couldn't even work out what she was looking at. The shape would become a shadow or trick of the light, and then nothing at all.

The starlight gleamed coldly on the hard stone contours of the buildings, and Amber shivered and pulled the zip up further on her hoodie as the damp chill in the air ate into her.

She glanced across the street to the brick wall on the other side. For a moment she imagined that someone stood there. But in fact it was nothing more than a drawing of someone, daubed on the wall in paint. Large black eyes stared out from the oversized head and long arms stretched across the dirty brickwork. It looked more like an alien than a human. *Didn't I meet some kind of alien creature once?* Amber thought. *Somewhere in the Emptiness?*

As that idea flittered around in her head, Amber decided that maybe the pit-like eyes had become larger and deeper, as if her fear had somehow stretched or magnified them. Hurriedly she looked away from the drawing. The seemingly mad notion that this hellish image could detach itself from the wall and chase after her would not leave her thoughts.

Amber walked from street to street at random and stopped occasionally to look up at the silent, empty high-rise blocks. She thought that she recognised some of the streets, but the way they joined onto one another was somehow wrong, as if this part of the city had been cut into pieces like a jigsaw and the pieces moved around. Amber imagined the hundreds, maybe even thousands of empty, unfurnished apartments in the abandoned blocks, the long dark corridors and stairwells, and she shuddered.

At one point she came across an open area of grassland and thought she recognised the indistinct black shapes of the buildings beyond. Wasn't one of them a school, and another one a police station? She stopped by the fence that separated the area from the road, and for a moment wondered if she ought to make her way across the grass. But a nagging fear stopped her. She felt certain that if she walked that way she might start to sink into the ground, as if the fabric that held this world together existed only weakly there.

"Don't be stupid," Amber scolded herself, but she couldn't bring herself to walk into that deeper darkness.

She continued along the street and eventually reached an area that looked familiar. A library that she and her dad had visited a couple of times stood here, alongside a few sorry-looking shops- that she recognised. A little convenience store and a takeaway called Quality Kebabs which had recently been condemned as unfit to serve food. Someone had shot one of the windows, Amber recalled, and when she looked she saw the hole in place in the glass.

Amber guessed that the low grey and brown building that housed the library had been built in the nineteen-seventies or maybe even earlier. It looked even more hideous than the other buildings nearby, as if someone had shoved together a load of blocks that didn't fit properly. The entrance door stood wide open, and at least half of the lights were on inside. Amber stopped and wondered if the lights made the place safer or not. For one mad moment she felt as if she had to decide which were good and which were evil- the distant stars above, or the electric lights of civilisation.

Minus the civilisation, Amber reminded herself, and wondered why she hadn't fully stopped thinking of the world in simple terms of good and evil. *Stop being a little girl,* she told herself sharply.

She approached the building and then made her way cautiously inside, past the unoccupied reception desk and down one of the aisles. The warm air made for a welcome relief from the chilly night outside. *This really is the library,* she thought suddenly. *Did I find my way back without knowing? Have I left the Emptiness?*

Amber stopped to look at a few of the books. Some had been placed in a large box at the end of the aisle, marked "For Sale". She looked inside three of the books and discovered that they were only twenty pence each, but judging by the fact that the box was full none of the books had been taken. *No one even bothers to steal books from libraries these days,* Amber thought as she put them back, *so it's hardly surprising that no one will pay for them either.*

"Are you all right, dear?"

Amber squealed and almost jumped out of her skin. She whirled round and saw an old woman peering worriedly at her. She had thick, large glasses with pink frames and wore a light blue cardigan. She leaned on an old book trolley and had a book in one hand, which she then put back on a nearby shelf.

"I... I'm... I don't know," Amber said helplessly. "I mean, I... I thought I was somewhere else..." She glanced around the library and suddenly noticed how real and mundane everything seemed. *I'm back,* she thought, astonished. She couldn't see anyone else, but she could hear a couple of low conversations including someone talking about opening hours to a member of staff at the reception desk. "Do you not open on Saturdays now?" she heard. "No, unfortunately we just don't have the staff available to cover, and we've had to make cutbacks," came the reply. "It's the same story everywhere," the customer remarked sadly.

Everything appeared and sounded quite normal. Had she imagined the last few hours of her life?

"Would you like to sit down? You look quite pale." The woman gestured to a seat across from her. "Oh, I am sorry," she added regretfully as Amber walked over and sat down, shaking. "I didn't mean to scare you. It's just you looked lost. Do you live round here?"

"Um... yeah. Fairly close," Amber said. She felt embarrassed, but also a little bit unnerved. Why did it matter where she lived? "I ought to get back," she added, but the warmth of the library had sapped her energy.

Rain started to pelt down outside. It lashed at the windows as if desperate to break them, and it reminded Amber of the storm when she and Joe had been left in Patrick's cottage a year and a half ago. Her dad and Emma had gone with Patrick to stand against the Order, in the belief that they had caused the storm. They had told her and Joe to stay in the house. But they never came back, or rather they probably did only to find that she and Joe had disappeared. Joe took them both into the Emptiness...

Amber quickly crushed that thought and the unsettling image that had started to form in her mind. *I remember that bit more than I want to,* she thought. *That blackness coming through the ceiling from the room above. It's what happened afterwards that's still murky.*

"There there, dear," said the librarian, patting her on the shoulder. "Are you sure you're all right? You look so pale. I think sometimes you youngsters just don't eat enough, and that's why you feel so... what's the right phrase? Spaced out? I'm afraid I'm not familiar with all these modern phrases..."

Amber let the old woman prattle on, barely listening. But at the same time the feeling of unease inside her steadily grew. She looked at the woman's cardigan and for a moment she felt certain that she had seen it before somewhere.

Odd, horrifying thoughts took root in her mind. She imagined that the librarian was much faster and stronger than she appeared and could run after anyone who stole books and punish them. A bizarre image came to her of limbs that stretched and snapped to reform themselves as the old woman-prepared to hunt down and eat the book thieves while they were still alive.

"Let me fetch you something to eat," she heard the librarian say, and the words somehow pulled Amber back into her situation.

"It's a library," she said automatically and forced herself to look the old woman in the eyes. "You can't eat in the library."

"Really?" The librarian's smile was one of genuine amusement. "But I eat here all the time. Who's going to stop me?" She leaned forward a little and Amber recoiled as she glimpsed something small and dark move inside her mouth. "I have my lunch here and then I go home for dinner." The old woman's voice had become oddly breathless, with a tremble to it. "I am *so hungry* sometimes. I wish people would stay for dinner. I wish they would stay." The last few words were uttered in a low, desperate moan.

The harsh ceiling lights had dimmed around their edges, as if an unknown gloom worked its way into them from the surrounding ceiling tiles. *Here comes the darkness,* a voice whispered in Amber's head. *It seeps through anything and everything.* "Well, *I* need to go back home," she said quietly.

"It's raining," the librarian pointed out.

"I don't care if it's raining." Amber got up and took a couple of steps towards the library entrance. But the old woman said something in a sharp tone that stopped her immediately.

"You can't go *home,* Amber. You know perfectly well that you don't *have* one anymore. Home's gone. Daddy's gone. Joe's *long* gone."

Amber froze still. *Joe,* she thought miserably, and as if she'd spoken his name the old woman sighed and continued, "Ah, Joe. Gone forever from your dreary life, but he lingers on in your head, doesn't he? Like a footprint or a ghost. A faded sketch of the boy you once knew."

Amber could say nothing, so consumed was she with fear and grief.

"All you have is us. You really do have to accept that this is the way things are. The rain comes and goes, even the stars themselves and the worlds that spin around them come and go over time, but *we* are forever."

Amber felt something begin to prickle inside her hands and all along her spine. It felt like an attack of pins-and-needles except that it moved back and forth as a wave of energy that made its way around her body. *What's happening to me?* she thought desperately, but a part of her already knew. It was the same feeling she had when the creatures of the Order burst through the door of her apartment.

She felt as if she had finally woken up from a dream which had lasted her entire life. *My powers wake,* she thought, and those words echoed around in her head, their truth amplified with each moment that passed. *I learned the truth about the world and now I face my own inner truth.*

That's where the light came from when the Order found us before.

When she finally turned to face the librarian, Amber already knew that she would see someone- or something- quite different to a benign old lady. Her enemy would show its true face.

Even so, the transformation shocked her.

The librarian looked much thinner now, her wrinkled skin drawn close over the bones of her face, her eyes sunken and red-rimmed. Her thick, yellow nails tapped meaningfully on the nearby book trolley. The blue cardigan hung off her skinny frame as if it had been casually thrown onto her. Her mouth, which hung slightly open, revealed two rows of tiny, sharp teeth.

"Aren't you tired of running away?" the creature enquired. Its voice sounded somehow thick, distorted and *wet,* as if it spoke through an invisible layer of mud. A dense musty odour like damp earth and old bones hung in the air. "You've no one left, Amber. It doesn't matter whether you're here or back where you came from. You're on your own now, and forever more. Oh, yours will be such a *lonely* life."

The creature tilted her head to one side like a grotesque, inquisitive bird and gave Amber a sly look.

"Unless you join us, of course. Then you'll have a family forever."

Amber swallowed and fought down her urge to scream. "I'm... I'm not scared of you," she managed to say.

"Aren't you, dear? Well then, why does your voice shake so much?" The bony creature looked her up and down contemptuously. "Do you know what I think? I think you want to be a big girl, all grown up and brave, but you're not really like that at all. You're just a silly, frightened child who's way out of her depth and doesn't know what to do."

"I know what you are," Amber said as another memory loomed suddenly in her head. She and Joe had found an abandoned village in the Emptiness, and in that village they'd found an unoccupied house. The two of them had walked into that house, ate food and left. But then an old woman had called to them as they left the village. They had ran as fast and as far as they could...

"We've met before," Amber whispered. "You're... one of them."

"One of *them*? What's that supposed to mean, dear?" The creature looked contemptuously at her. "I'm one of the Free. That's what you meant to say, wasn't it?"

Amber couldn't say anything at all, and the old woman grinned. "You're a clever girl in some ways, Amber. But you're not so good at thinking for yourself, are you?"

"I know all about you. About the Order. I learned about that from..." Amber stopped herself just in time, but the creature flashed a toothy, cunning grin. "From your daddy? Well, he's gone now. It's just you and me." She crept a little closer, her eyes fixed on Amber the whole while. "You should have stayed for dinner when you and Joe came to my house before. We could have had a nice little chat, the three of us. I could have explained to you how things *really* work. The secrets of all the worlds would have opened up for you. But you ran away, didn't you? You stole my food and then you ran away. So *rude* of you both. That wasn't very nice, was it?"

"No," Amber whispered. She couldn't help but stare into the merciless pits of the creature's eyes and the savagery that burned there. "It wasn't very nice."

"So maybe we should make things right, what do you think? We could have that little chat now. It's a shame Joe's not here, but that can't be helped. You and I have a lot of things to talk about. We have much more in common than you might think."

Amber blinked, suddenly aware that her enemy had managed to get much closer to her. *How did she do that?* she wondered as she stumbled backwards.

Then the creature reached out with long-nailed fingers, and the power that surged and prickled within Amber immediately bubbled to the surface. Strange words emerged from her mouth, words she had never heard before and wouldn't remember afterwards. The creature gasped in shock and pain and swayed on its feet for a moment, then threw Amber a look of utter malevolence. Amber saw its lips move as if her enemy silently uttered something, and for a moment she felt an invisible weight press against her, foul and searching. The protective shield which her words had created rippled and then threw back her enemy's unseen force.

The creature wiped at the blood that now trickled from its mouth. It no longer even remotely resembled a human being. The skin that remained on its face looked tight and pinched, as if drawn inwards by an invisible force. Its eyes were a stagnant yellow, feral and filled with madness.

Her attack on the creature had at least broken the spell that it had put Amber under. She could feel her powers rush through every part of her now. Her enemy snarled at her, all attempts at persuasion now abandoned. But then, instead of leaping at her it took a couple of steps backwards. *It's afraid of me,* Amber thought suddenly, and a rush of exhilaration went through her. *This thing is actually afraid of me!*

You can destroy it, a calm and certain voice whispered in her head. Amber concentrated and felt her powers reach out towards the beast. Its eyes widened in fear, then it turned and fled. A ripple of energy surged after it, but too late. The creature rounded a corner in the distance and the power that Amber had set loose instead slammed into a bookshelf and cut straight through a line of books. A moment later she heard a door open and close in the distance.

Amber remained too shocked to even move for a while afterwards. She listened intently but could hear absolutely nothing. Whoever or whatever the other occupants of the library had been, they had now fled as well. *It's all right,* she told herself, trying to calm her racing heart. *It's all right for now, anyway.*

After a while she made her way up to the bookshelf that had borne the brunt of her attack. It looked as if a red-hot poker had been pushed at high speed straight through the books and the shelf on which they stood. A smoking hole had been torn straight through them and even damaged another bookshelf further away afterwards. *I did that,* she realised, both fascinated and frightened. *I've woken up at last. Dad told me it would happen someday, but I didn't expect anything like this. I've no idea what I expected.*

Empowerment and fear battled for control inside her. But after a short while fear won the battle. Amber turned and ran from the library and the mad flicker of its lights, and almost flung herself into the waiting darkness of the cold and empty city.

JOE

1

Joe stood with his hands in his coat pockets and gazed across the park as the sun slipped below the tree line in the west. The long shadows that stretched across the grass suddenly disappeared and a quiet, wintry gloom spread in moments. In the places where the trees provided shelter from the sunlight the frost had remained all day.

The almost perfect silence of the late afternoon made him uneasy, but that wasn't unusual. Joe often thought that this little town felt *too* quiet, as if it silently hated its own humdrum existence.

Something happened, he thought miserably for maybe the hundredth time that day. *Something happened to Amber.*

Yesterday evening he had suddenly had a panic attack and cried out her name, certain that she was in danger. It wasn't the first time he had suffered a panic attack, but this one had felt different, as if something had connected him more strongly to Amber for a moment, but not enough to help her.

He shivered unhappily, dug his hands even deeper into his pockets and walked on up the road. He felt colder than ever and not just because of the damp chill in the air. Something that he could only describe as icy despair worked its way a little further into him. He had never felt quite so wretched and helpless before.

Joe had hated Westerton since the day of their arrival, and nothing had happened to change his opinion. It had been a bad idea for Emma to rent a house here, and he had told her two days after they arrived. Since then he had reminded her many times, but Emma had insisted that they had to stay here awhile longer. Joe couldn't recall her ever explaining *why* they needed to.

Emma had devised a carefully made story about her being his mother, backed up by the fake documents that she had needed when he started at the school. She had even had passports made for them both which looked completely genuine as far as Joe could tell- not that they had ever tried to get through Border Control. *Sometimes I wish we had,* Joe had thought gloomily more than once. *That way either we'd just be arrested, or if we got lucky we might end up someplace where we wouldn't have to worry about our enemies. If such a place exists.*

But it didn't, of course. Their enemies were everywhere. The world would surely have been in a bad enough state without them, but the Order had made everything even worse, amplifying racial tensions, wars over territory, the use of organised religion to control and subvert people, and generally doing everything possible to make humanity angrier and more hateful than ever before. It had been easy for them to spread misinformation and fake news. Emma had tracked a simple meme that someone could have put together in five minutes, and had shown him how it quickly reached over a hundred thousand people, many of whom then found ways to leap on the message behind it and amplify the twisted message further.

"The facts matter less each day," she had said. "And when people no longer care about facts..."

Joe had completed that unfinished sentence several times. *When people no longer care about facts, the most convincing liars seize control. When people no longer care about facts, they let their emotions control them. When people no longer care about facts, hate spreads like a virus.*

All the Order had to do was say the right things to the right people and let human nature do the rest.

As far as everyone else in the village knew, his name was Jamie. But Joe suspected that most of the nosey, suspicious-minded people in the village either knew that that wasn't his real name or that there was something "not quite right" about him and Emma. On top of that, a lot of the kids here were a bit stuck up. Many of them were driven to school, usually by their mums in huge four-by-four type cars with tinted windows. Joe would have felt like an outsider here even if he hadn't known all the things that he knew about himself and Emma and the Order. But with terrible secrets forever swarming in his head, he felt not so much an outsider as a visitor from another planet.

He hadn't made any friends, but then he hadn't tried to. *We won't be here for long anyway,* he had told himself many times. *Sooner or later something will happen, or Emma will get suspicious about something, and we'll have to move on. We always do.*

As he walked on up the street towards his house he saw Dean Michaels, a boy from his class, walking down the other way towards him. A thin boy with scruffy dark hair which he mostly kept under an old beanie hat, Dean was normally fairly quiet- even quieter than Joe- and Joe expected him to shuffle past without even saying anything. But instead he stopped.

"Guess what?" he said quietly.

Joe hated it when people said that. He wondered why Dean couldn't just tell him whatever he wanted to say.

"What?" he asked wearily.

"I found something in the woods. I haven't told anyone else. You'll *never* guess."

Joe didn't even think of guessing. His first instinct was to wonder why Dean had decided to tell *him*. Had he decided to speak to whoever he saw first, no matter who that might be? That didn't make sense. *Sometimes it feels like I'm the only person in this village who can keep secrets,* Joe thought. *I've had plenty of practice after all. Everyone else loves to discuss other people's business. Maybe I come across as someone who can keep a secret and that's why he told me. But if I was him I wouldn't tell anyone at all. Why risk it?*

"Have a guess then." Dean stared impatiently at him and then shivered suddenly as a gust of wind blew across the street.

"A dead body?" Joe shrugged. Immediately he wished he'd said something a little less strange. "I'm only joking," he added hastily.

Dean appeared not to have heard him. "It's a hole. One that goes *really* deep. I threw some stones and bits of wood into it and I couldn't hear them afterwards."

A chill came over Joe although he couldn't say why. "It's probably a sinkhole," he heard himself say. "They can be pretty deep. Anyway you should report it to the police, then they can make sure no one goes near it. Isn't your dad a police inspector? Why don't you tell him?"

Dean ignored the questions. "Don't you want to see it first?"

"I have to get back home. My... mum said I need to help with a few things."

Joe hurried on up the street. "Bye," Dean called out, and Joe half-turned and waved, but Dean had already started to walk the other way, head bowed as he hurried home through the chilly dusk.

Joe's concentration suffered even more than usual that evening. He sat in his room and tried to do his homework, which always proved difficult because he knew that ultimately there was no point to it. No number of school qualifications would ever fix his life. He only did the work to avoid getting into trouble and drawing attention to himself, but he never found it easy to focus on it.

After a while his thoughts returned to the hole in the ground that Dean had mentioned. A hole he couldn't even be sure existed until he went to look for himself.

Why should I care whether it exists or not? he asked himself, oddly frustrated. *I should remember what Emma always tells me and stay away from trouble.*

Eventually he gave up, put his work to one side and sat back in his chair, still trying to puzzle it out. *Why would Dean make up something like that? And if it is real, then why would he tell me about it? I don't even know him that well. I wouldn't say we were friends. I don't really have any friends in this stupid place. What's the point in trying when I have to move somewhere else every three months or less? In fact what's the point in doing anything at all?*

I'll never be able to have a normal life. I'll never feel safe.

Suddenly he felt angry at everything. His old life had become nothing more than a distant memory, a time that may as well have never existed. Things could never go back to the way they were. He could sense himself becoming more paranoid and uneasy on an almost daily basis, and he could do nothing about it.

Joe had wondered if he might miss Amber less over time. He didn't want to, but he worried that she would gradually fade from his life. It hadn't worked out that way though. He missed her now more than ever. Not having any idea where she might be made it unbearable, particularly as he still sensed her faint presence.

And so, his sudden, desperate panic, that dread certainty that something had happened to her, was impossible to deal with.

But even worse was the fact that now he couldn't sense her at all.

That same afternoon Dean had gone straight upstairs to his room as soon as he arrived back. He had a lot to think about, and no idea how to deal with it or where to even start.

When his dad suddenly opened the door he jumped, startled. Dean hadn't even heard him come upstairs even though most of the steps always creaked loudly. *That's happened a lot recently,* he reflected. *He's become more silent and more scary at the same time.*

"We need to have a little chat," his dad said. "Downstairs in five minutes."

Dean sat down on the small sofa in the living room a little later. His dad sat in the larger one opposite, leaned back and watched him for a short while with his cold, hard blue eyes. To Dean they always looked the same- angry but in a controlled way.

"I need you to do something," his dad said finally. "I think you'll find it easy enough. There's a boy called Jamie Richards in your year. You know who he is, don't you?"

Dean nodded reluctantly, but at the same time he felt his skin crawl as fearful questions chased one another through his mind. Had his dad somehow found out about the hole in the woods? Did he already know that Dean had mentioned it to Jamie?

I should have kept my mouth shut, he thought angrily. *I can usually do that without any problem, so why did I have to start blabbing about what I'd be found? Just because I wanted to talk to him?*

"I need you to keep an eye on that boy for me. Make friends with him."

Dean felt completely taken aback, and he became more certain than ever that something was very wrong. "Keep... an eye on him? Is he in trouble?" he asked eventually. "Shouldn't that be a matter for the police if he needs watching? I mean, I'm not answering back," he added hastily when his dad just stared at him with a horrible empty look in his eyes. It was that detached, almost bored look that he always had when he hit people. "I just meant, maybe the police are better at doing that sort of thing." Dean's father was- as Joe had pointed out earlier- a detective inspector in the local police force.

"Are you being difficult, Dean?" His dad leaned slowly forward, and Dean shrank back a little further into the sofa. He hated cringing like a little boy (after all, he wasn't being threatened exactly, not on *this* occasion) but he couldn't help but react this same wretched way each time. Every movement caused Dean to feel a little stab of fear whenever his father was in this sort of mood.

"No," he said quietly. "I just thought it would be..."

"Never mind what you thought it would be. I have asked one simple thing of you. You're not going to let me down, are you?"

"He keeps himself to himself," Dean said. "I spoke to him today actually, but he... he just doesn't say much. I don't think he even *wants* friends."

Dean's dad tightened his lips in an expression of disapproval. "That's *very* disappointing, Dean, seeing as you haven't even tried yet. Maybe everyone in your school needs to learn about your diary. Supposing if some of the pages from it found their way onto social media. How would you cope with that, do you think?"

Dean couldn't answer. Deep down he had known that the diary would be mentioned sooner or later. He felt so hopeless and full of despair that his eyes filled with tears which then began to roll down his cheeks.

"*Badly,* I think is the word you might be looking for. Remember, once information is on the Internet it's virtually impossible to remove it. Data spreads like a virus. You'll be... what's the word? *Trending.*"

I hate you so much, Dean almost said then, but he stopped himself just in time. He wished he could just sink right back in the furniture and disappear forever, swallowed up and pulled through into some other place where no one else could go.

"All you have to do is be friendly and see what you can find out. It should be easy work for you. After all..." His father gave a little laugh. "You do prefer *boys*, don't you Dean?"

Dean had already known the words that were coming, but the misery and shame still almost overwhelmed him. "Okay. I'll try," he managed to say. His voice trembled so much that he could barely get the words out at all.

"Try hard," his dad said. "For your own good. Oh dear," he added with sudden mock concern. "You've started to *cry,* Dean. Are you all right?"

Dean tried to reply but couldn't. Finally he just shook his head.

Then, to Dean's surprise his dad leaned forward and stretched out his hand. "Let's make a deal. You do a good job for me and I'll keep your sordid little fantasies away from everyone."

After a moment's hesitation Dean shook his dad's hand. It occurred to him a moment later that he had never shaken hands with him before in his life. His hand itched for a short while afterwards and he scratched absently at it. It felt as if a small electric charge had touched him at the same time.

Dean didn't eat much of his dinner that evening. He forced down the little that he could stomach and barely tasted it. As usual, neither of his parents said anything to him or to each other, their cold silence broken only by the harsh clatter of cutlery. Afterwards, after being excused he went back upstairs to his room.

Without thinking, he opened the top drawer of his bedside table, only to find it empty. This was the drawer where he had kept his diary, but his dad had confiscated it a week ago and there was no chance that he might give it back. The look of disgust on his parents' faces after they'd found out about it had been bad enough, but his dad had made it even worse by reading out parts of it to his mum. She had even begged him to stop at one point, but he had just laughed and carried on.

That's what he does whenever she begs him to stop, Dean thought hatefully as he slammed the drawer shut, and immediately feared that his father had heard the noise. *No matter what it is. He just laughs and carries on.*

"They never loved me anyway," he said. "It doesn't matter what they think."

But somehow it *did* matter, even though it shouldn't.

Dean wished more than anything that he hadn't written down any of the feelings that had been going through his head for a year or more. All the diary had done was make things far, far worse than they needed to be.

I wish I was older, he thought. *Then I could leave home and never go back or have to worry about what they think.*

But no. Like the idiot I am, I had to write things down in a diary.

One day he had just forgotten to hide it away, and his dad had found it. Since then he had kept it somewhere secret, probably locked away. Alan Michaels was a man who prided himself on his great attention to detail and thoroughness. Dean wouldn't have been surprised if his father had scanned all the pages and kept multiple copies on a secure cloud storage account somewhere.

He sighed and sat at the desk he used for homework. *I suppose it could have been worse,* he thought after a while. *All he's asked me to do is spy on someone. If Jamie doesn't mind hanging out with me sometimes it shouldn't be a problem.*

Dean felt ashamed of himself though. He would have liked to hang out with Jamie regardless. He liked him. He seemed cool, different somehow. Now he felt as if he was about to do something terrible, and the fact that it was someone he liked made it worse.

"Just do it," he told himself quietly. "Just do it. You know what will happen if you don't."

He hardly slept at all that night. Sometime in the small hours he gave up trying to sleep altogether. He lay in bed with dark thoughts swimming around in his head, as the morning came and the objects in his room came slowly into view.

2

Joe went out for a walk after breakfast the following morning, even though it was even colder outside than it had been yesterday. Today was Saturday, which meant relief from the relentless stress of school, not that weekends were much use around here. Westerton had the park, a huddle of useless shops like nail salons and party planners on the high street, two pubs, a church and a social club which was about to close down, and that was that.

Still, he had found that walking helped him think matters through even if it couldn't change anything. At least it was a bright sunny day.

He saw Dean standing by himself outside the convenience store in the high street. He looked anxious about something, Joe thought as he approached. When Joe reached him, Dean asked quietly, "Hey Jamie. Do you want to come and see this hole in the woods?"

"I don't know." Joe looked doubtfully at him. Dean looked almost desperate. "Are you okay?" he asked on an impulse.

Dean looked taken aback by the question. "Um... yeah. I guess. Well?"

"I suppose I don't have anything better to do," Joe admitted reluctantly. Maybe if he went and had a look at this mysterious hole then Dean might stop bothering him about it. Maybe he could even convince him to tell his dad about it.

As long as he keeps me out of this whole business afterwards, Joe thought as he remembered Emma's daily reminders to him to keep a low profile. She had said the same thing to him this morning that she always did. *Keep your eyes open. Be careful who you speak to and what you say. And always think before you speak.*

He walked with Dean across the village common and into the woods. As they pressed on deeper into the thickness of the trees and the light dimmed, Joe recalled the time when he and Amber had walked through a different woodland, next to the town where they had lived. It had been the summer then, the days hot and the nights stiflingly humid. *I couldn't sleep properly then either,* he reflected, *but it wasn't just because of the heat. Someone or something tried to reach me. The Guardian. That's how it all started...*

He banished the thought and shuddered as he felt the cold breeze eat into him a little more. He could remember only fragments of the events that had happened at that time and the idea that he might suddenly recall more without any warning frightened him. *I really don't need anything else to deal with,* he thought.

Less than a year and a half had passed since the blur of the Emptiness and the dreamlike events that had happened to him and Amber, but to Joe it could have been a lifetime. The events of that time felt almost as if they had happened to someone else.

As they walked, Joe glanced at Dean and wondered why he was so quiet today. He hadn't said anything at all since they'd left the village. He just looked glumly ahead as if the journey was a chore he had to get through.

"Are you all right?" Joe inquired after a while. Dean's morose silence had started to unnerve him.

"Yeah. Fine. You already asked me," said Dean. "It's just up ahead," he added, and a moment later the path opened out into a clearing of short grass. The ground had subsided in the middle. Joe tentatively walked as near as he dared to the edge, peered over and then stepped back.

"I wonder what's down there," he said.

"Nothing."

Joe looked across at him. "Well there has to be something at the bottom. Earth or rock, whatever. Doesn't there? It can't go on forever."

Dean took a small stone from his pocket. "Listen," he said, and tossed the stone into the middle of the hole. The two boys listened intently. Joe couldn't hear anything except the faint sigh of the breeze in the trees and the rustling of the grass. The stone didn't make any sound at all as far as he could tell. Finally, after about a minute had passed and still he hadn't heard any sound from inside the hole, he said quietly, "I didn't hear anything."

"No. Neither did I. And when I came here before I threw a bigger stone in. That didn't make any sound either. It was like it just got swallowed up and that was it."

As if the stone disappeared, or when it fell into the hole it also fell through a different world, Joe thought. He shivered and took another step back as the faint memory of the gateway in the Emptiness whispered in the back of his mind. He recalled a dark space in a vast cavern, but almost nothing about the people and creatures that had gathered to watch.

"I'm going to take a photo," Dean said, and took his phone out of his pocket.

"You didn't do that already then?" Joe was surprised.

"No. Didn't think to." Joe watched as Dean held his phone out and took a few careful steps forward, trying to compose the picture. "How come you don't have a phone?" Dean asked him suddenly.

"I... how do you know I don't have one?" Joe replied. At the same time he checked the inner pocket of his coat to make sure his pay-as-you-go phone was still there. Emma had given it to him months ago so he could contact her in an emergency. No one else knew the phone existed. In fact it was pretty useless for everything except calls. It had one contact listed and that was Emma. It couldn't even browse the Internet after Emma had locked it down. The two of them had had a huge argument about that, more of a shouting match really. Joe had felt so exhausted afterwards that he wanted nothing more than to sleep and make the world go away. Although he hadn't realised at the time, the confrontation had affected Emma just as badly.

Dean took a photo, swore and took another one. Joe noticed that his hands shook slightly. "Um... I've never seen you use one, that's all. It doesn't matter." He shoved the phone back into his jeans pocket, strangely distracted. Joe thought for a moment that he heard an odd sighing sound, like the wind in the trees but somehow more *human*. The air felt warmer for a moment. *What just happened?* he wondered uneasily.

Joe thought Dean said something else to him then, but for some reason he couldn't understand the words. When he turned to ask Dean what he had said, Joe froze to the spot, terrified by what he now saw.

Dean had *two shadows*.

One shadow lay exactly where it ought given the position of the sun. The other lay at a right angle to it, and otherwise looked exactly the same. When Dean moved, both shadows also moved.

Joe tried to speak but he couldn't. He couldn't even move. His world had ground to a terrifying halt.

"What's the matter?" he heard Dean ask. The voice seemed to come to him from far away. "Jamie?"

Joe felt a hand tentatively touch his shoulder, and he jumped, startled. He blinked and saw Dean peer at him. Everything suddenly seemed louder and brighter, as if the wind had intensified and the sun had become stronger.

"I... I'm fine." He looked down at the grass and saw that the *wrong* shadow had disappeared. The other moved as it ought. *What about mine?* he thought suddenly, and looked hastily down. But he only had one, and it was in the right place.

I imagined it, he thought, and tried desperately to stop shaking. *If it was real it would still be there. So I just imagined it. How can anyone have two shadows when there's only one sun?*

But an answering thought came quickly. *Remember when you thought you imagined things before? They turned out to be real, didn't they? Not quite in the way you expected, but they were still real.*

Even Amber thought you might be going mad at first.

"Are you sure? You look like you're going to vomit or something."

"We ought to go back," Joe said abruptly. "This hole is really deep. It's dangerous. We need to tell the authorities and get this whole place cordoned off like I said to you. We shouldn't even be here. Why don't you just tell your dad about it?"

Dean didn't appear to have heard him. "Imagine what it would be like to fall forever," he murmured.

Joe stared at him. "You wouldn't fall forever. That's impossible. You'd have to stop eventually."

"The stones didn't. Maybe they're still falling now."

"What, right through the centre of the earth or something?" Joe found himself getting irritated by the whole argument. He desperately wanted to get away from this place, and not just because he had started to see things that weren't there. "They probably didn't make a sound you could hear because they landed in mud or soft earth or something far below," he said. "There's *always* a rational explanation."

Liar, a voice whispered in his head.

"Come on, let's go." Joe turned and strode off, and Dean followed after a moment.

When they reached the common again, Dean suddenly said, "Do you want to hang out somewhere tomorrow?"

65

"Um... maybe. I don't know." Joe felt a bit taken aback. Emma's words of warning echoed in his head again. *Keep your eyes open. Be careful who you speak to and what you say.* Then another, unpleasant thought occurred to him. What if he saw Dean's second shadow again? What if he saw something far worse? What if he then freaked out? That would be the end of his life as a fugitive.

"I'm just trying to be friends, Jamie." Dean's cheeks flushed red with embarrassment and he looked down at the ground.

"Okay. I don't have anything better to do," Joe admitted, for the second time in the day. He wondered if Dean was just lonely and desperate for a friend, and he recalled the boy's words from a short while ago‑ *Imagine what it would be like to fall forever.* Had he sounded depressed? Joe thought he might. "But promise me you'll tell your dad about that sinkhole in the woods this evening so it can be sealed off."

"All right." Dean sounded reluctant. *Doesn't he realise that someone could just fall in?* Joe thought. *Maybe someone already has. I'd be amazed if we were the only people who'd found it, after all there are people who walk their dogs in the woods every day. So why hasn't anyone else reported it yet?*

Joe wondered if maybe he should be the one to raise the alarm about the sinkhole. But he couldn't draw attention to himself.

"You live on Meadow Lane off the high street, don't you?" Dean said.

"Er... yeah." *How does he know that?* Joe asked himself uncomfortably. "I'll just meet you in the high

66

street, same place as today, outside the shop," he added hastily.

"Okay." Dean looked relieved. "Around midday?"

"I guess."

It was only a little later as he reached his front door that Joe wondered what he and Dean could possibly find to do in a dreary little village like Westerton, now that they'd seen the sinkhole.

I guess I'll find out tomorrow, he thought as he turned his key in the door.

That night Joe dreamed that he stood on the summit of a high mountain. It was night time and yet he could see land stretch out below in perfect detail- valleys, hills, woodlands, lakes and rivers, villages and towns.

He sat on the ground, oddly aware of time rushing past, although the night didn't turn to day. A cold breeze blew through the darkness, and he knew that it also blew through the silent, deserted streets of the ghost towns in the distance.

The world has changed, he thought. *Something terrible happened. But it had to happen, to stop something even worse.*

Someone or something whispered to him. Maybe the words came from inside his own head or maybe they were carried on the wind. *It was always going to end this way.*

"There's no hope," Joe said automatically, empty words that spilled out into the empty air.

For all that was? No. But you're still here.

"Why? Why am I still here?" At the same time he thought, *If I'm alone in the world, do I have any purpose at all? Do I make my own reason for existing?*

The voice wouldn't answer him. Some unseen creature or force of nature tried desperately to haul him upright and pull him away, and the words it uttered became a senseless, breathless rush.

Joe woke suddenly and sat up in bed. His heart raced. He recalled the last few parts of his dream but they became muddied and unclear in moments and faded away.

He got dressed and sleepily made his way downstairs. Emma had put one of the news channels on and was making some frantic, scrappy notes in a battered old notepad. Joe peered over her shoulder but couldn't read them. They looked like a weird kind of shorthand. Did *anyone* use shorthand anymore?

"Is that code for something?" he asked eventually.

Emma turned and blinked as if his question had confused her. "What? Oh, this?" She turned back to her scribbles. "Yes, it's a kind of code, Joe. An unbreakable one, I hope."

"I thought there wasn't any such thing," he called back as he wandered through to the kitchen to get some breakfast.

"There is if the code has no rules," Emma said. When Joe looked back through the doorway she was fully engrossed in the news once again, almost as if she was trying to decipher something about the current story, which was yet another report of mass slaughter in the Middle East. After a short while it cut to a scene of wide-eyed, screaming men firing guns in the air as if they had all lost control of themselves.

"I'm going out just before midday," he told her after he finished his breakfast and came to sit on the sofa. Emma frowned and looked at him, suddenly attentive. "Where?"

"Just out."

"Where and who with? Come on Joe. You know you need to give me that sort of information," she said when he responded with a deep sigh.

"I'm just hanging out with a boy in my class, that's all. I don't know where we'll go. Nowhere much, I expect. Where does anyone go round here?"

"And I assume this boy has a name?"

Joe hesitated. "Dean Michaels," he said reluctantly after a moment.

Emma looked thoughtfully at him. "Okay. Be careful what you say."

"Yeah, I know." Joe felt oddly relieved that she hadn't refused to let him go out. He was sure Emma knew that Dean's father was a police inspector. *Maybe I shouldn't go,* he thought suddenly, but he put the idea to one side. *Does Dean even know about that shadow?* he wondered suddenly, then told himself to stop being ridiculous. He had imagined it.

He was both embarrassed about and glad for his aunt's cautious attitude. If it hadn't been for their situation, and if he didn't know the truth about the way the world was, it would seem like paranoia. *But she's somehow kept us free for all these months,* Joe reminded himself as he set off down the road. *I don't know how, but she managed it.*

Dean was already by the shop when Joe walked down the street to meet him. He paced constantly up and down with his hands in the pockets of his coat and a scowl on his face as he stared at the pavement. *What is the matter with him?* Joe wondered.

"Shall we walk through the woods for a bit?" Dean blurted out as soon as Joe arrived.

Joe stared at him for a moment. "I... guess so," he said uncertainly. *Walk through the woods?* he thought, bemused. *Again? What for?*

They made their way across the grassy common in silence. Joe glanced across at Dean and wondered if he ought to think of something to say. But suddenly, just as they reached where the path went into the woods Dean stopped and turned to him.

"There's something I need to tell you," Dean said quietly. "I'm going to get into a hell of a lot of trouble for this, but I have to."

"Maybe you shouldn't," Joe said. In the back of his mind he heard one of Emma's quiet but sharp warnings again. *Stay away from trouble. Don't draw any attention to yourself.* "In fact, maybe you shouldn't have told me about that hole in the ground. Wait a minute. You haven't told your dad yet, have you?"

Dean didn't appear to have listened. "I don't have any choice," he continued. "I really don't have any choice. I can't do this."

Joe felt a chill stir within him. "Can't do what?"

"I've been thinking this over and over all morning and now I know what I have to do. It's really important. I just *know* it's important."

"You're not making any sense, Dean. I think I might just go back. I've got some things to do anyway..."

"Just *listen*." Dean looked furtively around and continued in a quieter voice, "My dad told me I had to keep an eye on you and tell him about whatever you do. Not that you've done anything I know of. I don't know why he asked me. I don't even *want* to know what he thinks you've done."

"I haven't done anything," Joe heard himself say. Instinctively he shrugged and tried to look puzzled, but his heart felt as if it had fallen through his stomach. He could feel his palms start to prickle with sweat even though the day was bitingly cold.

"No, well I don't really understand either. I mean, he could have got the police to do that, he *is* the police... you've got to understand, I didn't even want to, but he... well, he kind of blackmailed me." Dean looked more than embarrassed. He wiped his hair away to one side and looked away, blinking. Joe thought for a moment he might be about to cry.

"I've just had enough," Dean said eventually. His voice trembled. "I can't do this anymore, and I wanted you to know. None of it feels right. I couldn't do this to you, Jamie. Maybe now you can just carry on and *not* do whatever it was he thought you were going to do..."

Joe shook his head. "No. It's worse than that." Panic continued to build inside him. If Dean's father had got his son to spy on him, it could only mean one thing. He was a member of the Order.

Why hasn't he just captured me and Emma already? Joe wondered. *Is he waiting for us to do something? He must have some sort of plan!*

"I have to go," he muttered. He turned and began to walk quickly away, but Dean quickly caught up with him and grabbed his arm. "Wait! If we just pretend that I didn't tell you..."

"I *can't* pretend now that I know!" Joe pulled his arm free and broke into a run as he set off across the common. As he reached the road he threw a glance back to see if Dean had come after him, but he hadn't. He stood in exactly the same place as if he was too shocked to move, or maybe just horrified at what he had done.

3

Joe raced home. As soon as he got back he breathlessly told Emma everything that Dean had told him. Emma sat calmly after he had finished, although Joe could tell she was thinking frantically because she took her glasses off and began to polish them with a handkerchief. At the same time she stared into the middle distance and said nothing. This was how Emma thought things through in a crisis. Somehow he managed to wait silently for her to speak, but he couldn't help but pace restlessly around the living room. "Okay," she said finally. "We need to leave."

"Today?"

She turned to look at him and frowned. "When do you think, Joe? The middle of next week, perhaps?"

"I'm sorry... I just... I mean, you're right..."

Emma got up. "We're just lucky that Dean felt the way he did and told you, so at least we *may* have a bit of a head start. Get your things together, and then we'll drive up as far as Holmbridge and get the train from there. We'll have to hope he doesn't go and tell his father in the meantime. I don't expect he will, but behaviour is difficult to predict when someone's in a state of panic, which I expect he is."

"Where will we go?"

"I'll decide on the way. Hurry up. You've got ten minutes."

Joe ran upstairs. He had no real idea what to take with him, not that he had many possessions. After staring wildly around the room for a short while he grabbed his backpack and crammed some clothes into it. For a moment he stared at his school books on the shelf. *No,* he decided. *I won't be needing them. I probably won't need school books ever again.*

He quickly finished packing what little he had, slung his backpack over his shoulder and hurried downstairs.

Then they heard a knock on the front door.

"We have to hide," Joe whispered, but Emma shook her head. "I already know who it is."

"Who?" Joe demanded. But Emma went calmly through to the hallway and opened the front door. Joe followed her. When she opened the door, they saw Dean on the doorstep. Joe thought he looked like he was having a panic attack. Dean opened his mouth to speak but he didn't seem able to say anything. Joe's eyes caught a faint movement across the street, behind Dean's shoulder. One of their nosey neighbours peered from behind her curtains. *That's exactly what we don't want,* he thought desperately. The woman finally turned away but Joe imagined her already about to phone or text her friends. *Just seen something suspicious across the road... you know that woman and her son at number twenty-four, well I always thought there was something not quite right about them...*

Emma quickly ushered Dean inside. "So, you must be Dean," she said as she closed the door.

"You have to take me with you!" he blurted out as he stared at their backpacks. "You have to!"

Joe groaned in despair. "Dean, you're making things even worse! Just leave us alone and go home!"

"You don't understand. Please! When my dad finds out you've gone, I'll be punished. I mean, *really* punished. I *can't* stay. I have to come with you!"

"Well you can't! You've ruined everything!" Joe shot back, but to his bewilderment Emma said calmly, "Dean, come on through and sit down." She led him into the living room and Joe cast an agitated glance at the backpack he'd left at the bottom of the stairs as he followed them. "I thought we had to leave *now*," he muttered. "Maybe he's just trying to delay..."

"Be quiet," Emma said sharply. She motioned for Dean to sit opposite her. Then she sat down and said, "Give me your hands, Dean."

He just stared helplessly at her. "We haven't got much time," Emma continued, and when Dean still didn't respond she leaned forward and took both his hands, then closed her eyes. Dean looked helplessly at Joe, who shrugged. He'd never seen Emma do anything like this before. Was she using her powers in some way?

A sudden, horrible thought came to him. Could she be wiping part of Dean's memory? He felt as if he ought to feel relieved if she was, but the idea also made him ashamed- and a little afraid. He didn't see Emma's

76

powers at work very often, but when he did they were always a bit scary. He had seen her confuse someone and take away their short-term memory once before when they were in a desperate situation.

Finally she opened her eyes and nodded. "Yes. I thought as much. Dean will come with us," she said quietly.

Even as Dean stared wide-eyed at her and exclaimed "What?! Really?" Joe shook his head in disbelief. That was the last thing he had expected her to say. What was going on?

"You are joking!" he blurted out eventually.

"I'm most certainly not joking." Emma didn't turn to look at him. She still gazed steadily at Dean.

"Have you gone completely mad?" Joe exclaimed. "We *can't* bring him along! For one thing, it's kidnapping. It's a criminal offence. His dad will *never* stop hunting us if we do this! Sorry but *no way* am I..."

"I'll explain later, Joe." His aunt turned to look at him and he saw a hard, determined look in her eyes.

Dean looked at them both. "*Joe?* I thought your name was Jamie!"

"He doesn't have any stuff with him," Joe pointed out, ignoring Dean. "I'm not sharing my clothes with him! You keep telling me I don't think things through, but now you're doing *exactly*..."

Emma got up and walked over to Joe until she stood next to him. "Didn't you listen? I *said* I'll explain later. In the meantime I need you to grow up and do as you're told. There are certain things we must do, and I don't have time to explain them right now. This is

77

important. Dean is coming with us, and that's all there is to it. Do I make myself clear?"

She sounded as if she was making a big effort to control her anger. Joe couldn't remember the last time he had seen her like this. "All right," he said, taken aback. "Fine. Can we just get out of here?"

Emma quickly finished her own packing. Joe gazed around at the living room and kitchen, at how ordinary everything looked. He listened to the faint but irritating sound of the dripping tap over the kitchen sink. *We won't need to fix that now,* he thought. *Won't need to rinse out cups again, or boil the kettle or switch the TV on or anything else here. I won't need to do my homework or walk down the road to the school.*

He felt a sudden desperate desire for an ordinary life, however tedious and boring it might be. But that would always be an impossible dream.

Emma ushered them both out through the front door. She locked the door and then made her way down the path after them, unlocked the car and threw her backpack into the boot.

"Get in," she urged them. Joe got in the front, Dean in the back, and the three of them headed south through the village until they reached the main road. "We'll get the train and find somewhere to stay in the city for a short while," Emma said.

Joe was about to ask her where they would stay, but at the same moment Dean leaned forward and asked them, "Have the two of you done this before?"

"Three times already," Joe said.

"Wow." Dean looked from Joe to Emma and back again. "What is it you've done for the police to

78

want you so badly? Are you bank robbers or something? I mean, I don't care what you've done, I just want..."

"Do we look like bank robbers?" Joe shook his head. "Who even robs banks these days?" He paused and added, "We haven't done anything."

"Criminals can look like anyone." Dean paused and then added quietly, "That's what my dad always says. He says you have to be wary of everyone."

"Well he's right about that," Emma commented as she accelerated to overtake a lorry.

This whole thing is crazy, Joe thought dismally as he stared at the road ahead and rain began to patter against the windscreen. *Maybe Emma's gone a bit crazy as well. We'll definitely get caught this time, now we have Dean with us. Our luck has run out at last.*

They parked the car at Holmbridge train station. The boys hurried after Emma as she headed quickly towards the station entrance. *We keep leaving clues everywhere,* Joe silently noted as he looked back and shivered in the icy rain. *Our DNA will be all over that car.*

According to the departures screen, a train would leave for the city in four minutes. Emma bought tickets for the three of them. Luckily there was no queue at the ticket machines- and they got on the train which pulled in a minute early as they walked out onto the platform.

They managed to find a group of four seats together on the train. *All these trains have CCTV,* Joe glumly reminded himself as they sat down. *This has to be our dumbest escape yet.*

But at the same time he couldn't help but admire Emma's outwardly calm look. She appeared to be at least as relaxed as anyone else on the train. She certainly didn't look or behave like a fugitive. She just looked like a mum on a day out somewhere with her two boys. Joe looked across at Dean and saw somebody utterly lost in their thoughts, as if he didn't entirely believe what was happening around him and to him. *We shouldn't be doing this,* Joe thought uncomfortably. *We shouldn't have involved him in our miserable lives.*

The train departed on time and soon picked up speed once it pulled away from the station. Joe looked despondently through the window at the bleak wintry scene of bare, windswept trees and waterlogged fields and imagined himself being able to step outside the train, outside his entire existence. He imagined that he could run forever through the fields to some other, better life where no one pursued him, where he could exist without that horrible little knot of fear that was always there inside.

Stop it, he told himself wearily. *What have daydreams of a better life ever done for you?*

About ten minutes later the train rattled through two long tunnels. Joe felt pressure build slightly in his ears. He had noticed it before on a train as it went through a tunnel- and he swallowed to relieve it. *We'll be arrested near the ticket barriers when we get there,* he thought as his dismal reflection in the window stared back at him. *And that'll be the end of everything. I'm so tired of always having to hide, then run away, hide again then run away again. We may as well let them catch us.*

A short while later the train entered a third tunnel, and gradually slowed down until it came to a halt. After a moment, the driver's voice sounded over the intercom.

"Good afternoon ladies and gentlemen. I'd just like to apologise for the delay to this service. We're currently being held at a red signal waiting for a northbound train to clear the platform at Longfield station. Hopefully we'll be on our way shortly."

His words were followed by a pause, and then crackle and interference. At the same time Joe felt certain that the air became much colder for a moment. *What's happening?* he wondered, and he turned to Emma in order to ask if she knew.

But then the driver spoke again, this time a little more loudly.

"This is a message for the lady and two young boys sitting in coach number three. I'm afraid the train will remain here until you give yourselves up. All you need to do is walk forwards through the train to the guard's cabin. Knock on the door and you'll be allowed in. No tricks or it will end very badly for you all."

This is a nightmare, Joe decided as he stared helplessly at Emma. *It's just a nightmare and I'll wake up in a minute.*

Suddenly he remembered thinking the same thing when he and Amber had found themselves in the Emptiness a year and a half ago. He had thought *that* was a nightmare too, at first. But they hadn't woken up.

He looked slowly around and immediately saw the hostile stares of other passengers directed at them.

One old lady looked straight at him, her eyes cold and narrow with disapproval. A middle-aged man in a suit stared intently at Emma as if he was about to get up, walk over and punch her in the face. *We haven't done anything!* Joe felt like shouting at them.

The driver's voice crackled over the intercom again and made him jump. *"Well? What is there to think about? All you need to do is get up and walk. Do you really want to cause serious disruption to other passengers' journeys? Do you really think you can keep running away?"*

When none of them moved, the intercom fizzed and crackled more loudly than ever as if something nearby had caused interference. Again a wave of cold air washed over them before the temperature returned to normal.

Then a woman's voice spoke, and the words it uttered filled them with terror.

"Emma? Emma!" Whoever spoke sounded distant and desolate, as if she called up blindly from the bottom of a deep pit. *"Emma... please help me... it's so cold here... so cold and dark... please do as he says. I just want to go back..."*

Emma's face had turned ash-white. Her hands shook. But there was worse to come.

"Is that... is that Joe? My little Joe? It's been so long! Please help me... please... I'm falling forever..." Then the voice began to sob pitifully.

Oh my god, Joe thought in horror. *Is that my...*

He jumped suddenly as he realised that the old woman had moved and sat down again across the aisle from them. She leaned across with a crafty smile on her face. "You really should give up. It's for the best," she said, and Joe recoiled as he smelled a horrible odour on her breath. It was exactly the same smell he remembered from when he had got an infected ingrown toenail years ago. The woman's eyes were a dirty brown-yellow colour and her skin had a puffy, flushed appearance, as if everything just under her skin was diseased and had started to rot away. When she opened her mouth to speak again, Joe couldn't see any teeth at all, only a thick earthy brown tongue that rolled around inside her mouth.

"Don't you *want* your mother to be at peace?" she asked quietly. "How can she, if you keep running away? So *thoughtless* of you."

"We have to run," Joe whispered. His mouth felt as dry as dust.

The old woman shook her head, and Joe heard an odd scraping sound. "Don't be silly," she said, almost as if she was trying to comfort him. "You can't deny your own destiny. None of us can. You all have a place in the world, gifted as you are, but you need to take that first step."

As Joe listened and wondered why those words made so much sense, he suddenly heard Emma's voice cut through his muddled thoughts, softly commanding. "Don't listen to it, Joe. Don't look into its eyes. Turn away and look at me."

When he did so, Joe saw that Emma's eyes had become an intense, deep blue. He felt as if a leash had fallen away from around his neck and a weight lifted from his shoulders- a weight that he hadn't even realised existed.

The old woman swore loudly and spat on the carriage floor. "Well, *we* have eternity," she said distastefully as she moved further away. "How long do *you* have? How long are *you* prepared to wait?"

But then the driver suddenly screamed through the intercom, *"This has gone on long enough! Bring them to me!"*

The other passengers got up slowly and moved towards them at the exact same time. They appeared nervous but determined, as if spurred on by the driver's anger and impatience.

Emma stood up and raised both her arms, then moved them sideways quickly, and Joe stared in astonishment as all those people who had made their way towards them were flung back into the corners of their seats. They remained there in odd positions as if something invisible pinned them down and held them in place. Their eyes bulged and their faces grew red with fury. Some of them appeared to shout with rage, but Joe couldn't hear anything they said, as if Emma had made an invisible soundproof barrier between them.

"We need to get off this train," Emma said grimly, and she ushered them through the aisle towards the carriage doors.

"We can't step on the tracks," Joe heard himself protest. "Another train might come along, and the driver's probably stopped the doors from opening..." Then he noticed that the nearest set of doors had already opened. Had Emma done that when she threw their enemies back?

"There won't be any other trains." Emma
sounded certain. "Not here. Not in this place."

As Joe looked at her a cold feeling stirred in his
stomach. "What do you mean? Why not? Are we in…"

She shook her head. "Not exactly. We'll talk about it later. For now, we just need to get away from here. It won't be long until they break free, and I don't think I can hold them all back a second time. Not so soon."

A waft of cold damp air from the tunnel greeted them as they reached the doors. After they clambered down onto the loose stones by the side of the track, Joe looked back down the tunnel and saw the light of a lamp approach from some distance away. It swayed by itself in a sea of darkness. He heard someone or something mutter angrily although he couldn't make out any of the words. They might have been spoken in an alien language for all he knew.

"This way," Emma said urgently, and she led them back in the direction from which the train had come. The ballast stones crunched and slipped under their feet. Joe glanced up at the windows of the train carriages and saw faces pressed against the glass. Every single one stared at them with such undisguised hate that Joe couldn't look at any of them for more than a moment. They looked twisted and out of shape, as if distorted either by their rage or the strange hold that Emma's powers had over their movement. *The soldiers of the Order,* he thought numbly, and almost stumbled forwards. *How many of them know who they really answer to?*

He forced himself to look away and concentrate on the way ahead, although the gloom made it difficult. *Why couldn't we see them for what they were when we got on the train?* he wondered. *Surely either Emma or I ought to have sensed them? But now they show their true faces, as if their remaining humanity has melted away.*

"I'm going to wake up," he heard Dean whisper at his side. "I'm going to wake up. I'm going to wake up." The boy uttered those words in a breathless rush, as if by repeating them he might break out of this nightmare.

Suddenly Joe remembered the light they had seen further down the tunnel. He glanced back but saw only the dusty darkness. He recalled Emma's words from a moment ago. *There won't be any other trains.*

When they finally reached the mouth of the tunnel, Joe looked at his watch and saw that it was three o'clock and probably about to get dark soon. They walked up the grassy embankment and then Emma sat down with a faint sigh. She looked horribly pale and had started to shiver.

"What's happening?" Dean asked quietly. His voice trembled. He looked as frightened as Joe felt.

"I don't know," Joe replied weakly. He knelt down at Emma's side and held her hand. "Are you all right?"

"I will be," she murmured. "Just... need a minute."

"What did you do back there?"

Emma took a deep breath. "We... walked into their trap. I think something must have shielded them from us, which explains why we couldn't detect them. They were trying to take us all into the Emptiness, Joe. That's... what it was all about."

He stared at her. "That doesn't make sense."

"It doesn't," Emma agreed, "but I'm certain that that's what they did. They used up a lot of energy in trying to shield themselves and ensnare us. I think somewhere in that tunnel is a... a weak point between worlds, a place where it's possible to break through. An area that they could manipulate somehow."

Joe shook his head. "How could they possibly have known that we were on the train... oh." He stared meaningfully at Dean, who shrank back a little.

"I didn't tell him," Dean whispered. "I promise, I didn't tell anyone! I never even went back home!"

As Joe stared at the frightened boy, he suddenly remembered Dean's second shadow that he thought he had seen. *That was near the hole,* he thought. *Is that another place where the way between worlds is weak? Where does it lead?*

But that line of thought made him recall the terrifying words spoken by the voice that had pretended to be his mother. *Please help me... I'm falling forever...*

"You wouldn't have needed to," Emma said to Dean. "He would have figured it out sooner or later, once he discovered that we were gone and that you'd disappeared as well. I'm just surprised that this happened so quickly. His rank within the Order may be higher than I thought."

"He's a Detective Inspector," Dean said.

"I didn't mean his police rank." Emma rose unsteadily and looked back briefly into the tunnel. "We have to get away. Come on."

They made their way over a low fence at the top of the grassy slope and set off through the field that lay beyond, stumbling through the muddy twilight.

4

By the time they had walked through the countryside for half an hour or so the light had almost completely gone, but had reached the outskirts of small town.

Emma stopped outside a B&B as they walked down one of the streets and gazed at it for a moment. "This place will do," she said finally.

They walked through into the reception area. A young woman sat behind a desk, busy looking at something on her phone. She glanced up and put the phone to one side with a heavy sigh as if the three of them had ruined her evening. "We need a room for the night," Emma said.

"Um..." The young woman glanced at the boys and looked flustered.

"They're my sons," Emma said sharply. "Is that what you were about to ask me?"

"Wow. *Sorry.* I didn't mean to offend you." The receptionist's eyes widened and she gave them all a hurt look, as if to suggest that *she* was the one who had been offended. Then she got up and managed to spill some papers from her desk. "We have a room available," she said as she began to pick them up. They waited as she took one of the keys in the rack behind her. "Are you paying by..."

"Cash? Yes," Emma said. "How much?"

"Sixty pounds." The receptionist took the three twenty-pound notes that Emma handed over and made a show of holding each of them up to the light to check that they were genuine. Finally satisfied, she handed over the key and rattled through some information about the room and breakfast hours, which Joe barely listened to. *I just want to sleep and pretend today never happened,* he thought. *But I won't be able to. And what will tomorrow turn out to be like? Is that going to turn into a waking nightmare as well?*

The room smelled musty when they opened the door and stepped in. Emma opened the window and Joe listened to the oddly comforting sound of the traffic as he sat wearily on the edge of the bed. After a moment Dean sat next to him. He looked every bit as tired as Joe felt and his head slumped forward slightly. He glanced at Joe and said quietly, "I think I'm going mad. I can't wake up. Why can't I wake up?"

Dean looked so frightened and full of despair that on an impulse Joe put his arm around him. "It'll be okay," he lied.

Emma turned on the TV that had been set up in one of the top corners, and moved the chair away from the little desk before sitting down, so that she could see it better without craning her neck. "You two can have the bed," she said. "I'll just sleep here when I'm ready."

"Are you sure?" Joe asked.

"I could sleep anywhere right now. I'm sure the two of you could as well."

Joe watched as she selected one of the news channels, and recalled the cryptic notes she had made about the stories that the news channels ran- often in that strange code. As he watched the latest updates he observed gloomily that the news had become more packed than ever with wars, atrocities carried out by religious fanatics, natural disasters, planes crashing, ships sinking and civil unrest in many cities. Many of those cities were in countries he'd always thought of as quite peaceful. Was it even worse this week than last week? Joe thought so.

Everywhere in these news reports he saw angry, hate-filled faces, usually dozens or hundreds of them together. Often he saw religious preachers involved, lecturing their brainwashed followers and urging them on to ever greater acts of hatred. The looks he saw in everyone's eyes made him think they were all about to slip out of their human skins and become something else.

Just like the Order, he thought. *Are we all like them, deep down? What about Emma and myself, and Amber and Luke for that matter? Are we that different to everyone else? Sometimes it doesn't feel like it, no matter what we've experienced. Sometimes it feels as if we're just a few angry words away from being just the same as our enemies. Why is it so easy to hate?*

"It *is* getting worse," he commented after a while as they watched footage of violent protesters from two opposing groups fighting. He wondered why the police hadn't been there to keep them apart. Had they given up? Were there now simply not enough police to deal with everything that was going on? Or had they deliberately avoided the situation for some political reason? Perhaps the government had told them to let the carnage happen, so that they could make another emergency law. Three of those had already been passed this year.

Some of the people being helped away from the battle by their comrades clutched desperately at their faces as if they were trying to hold them together. Petrol bombs and bricks were being thrown. He saw people screaming, other people laughing. Sometimes it just sounded the same.

"The world's going to hell," he murmured.

"We're past the tipping point," Emma said. Joe wasn't quite sure what she meant by that, but the phrase made his skin crawl.

"But things will get better eventually, won't they?" Dean asked. He was already lying down on the bed and had his eyes closed. Joe had assumed he had fallen asleep.

"It depends what you mean by eventually," Emma said after a while. "Right now most people don't seem to be interested in things getting better. Their goal is the destruction of anyone who doesn't see the world the same way as them. *My truth is the only truth.*"

Dean didn't reply, but his eyes flickered open and he stared up at the ceiling for a long while. Joe thought he looked as miserable as he himself felt.

After a short while Emma spoke up again after looking round to make sure they were both still awake. "I may as well tell you this now, because it will soon become obvious anyway. Much of this is the work of the Order, whether directly or indirectly. I suspected as much for a while but now I'm certain of it. Events have made it easier for them, and they've seized the opportunity to make things even worse with problems that they created themselves. Politicians and military people have a phrase for it- a *perfect storm*."

"How do you know?" Joe asked.

"I recognise some of the people I've seen in the background in news reports. I've listened to the things that the newsreaders and reporters say. I've been trawling social media and forums and I've analysed what certain people have said. The Order have flooded the Internet with actual coded instructions to their followers. Now, those people themselves have followers. People who have never even heard of the Order. They just do as they're told, whether it's petty crime, stirring up hatred, whatever."

"So thousands of people are doing this?" Joe exclaimed.

"Millions, Joe, if you work your way far enough down the network."

"What is this *Order* you keep talking about?" Dean asked sleepily.

"I'll explain that when we get somewhere safer, where we can stay for a few days. Not here. I don't think I'd make a lot of sense right now anyway." Emma yawned and rubbed at her eyes.

"You said my dad was one of them," Dean reminded her.

"That's right. He is. That's why he told you to spy on Joe."

"And my mum?"

"Yes. Her too." Emma looked sympathetically at him.

Dean didn't reply for a moment. "Thought so," he said finally in a quiet voice, and Joe thought he sounded suddenly much younger than he had before. "She's just as bad. In a different way. Yeah, it all makes sense now. Sort of."

Dean suddenly turned over on his side, curled up and covered his face with one arm. Joe felt sorry for his companion, but he couldn't think of anything useful to say, so he turned back to Emma.

"That's what I don't understand," he began. "Why would he just *spy* on me? I mean, what did he expect me to do? Try to step back into the Emptiness again? And if he knew who I was, who we both were- why didn't he just have me arrested on some made-up charges or something? Why just... *observe* me like a creep?"

"I don't know. It could be that he expected something to happen, but I'm not sure what."

Dean sat up again and wiped at his eyes. "Step back into the emptiness? What's that supposed to mean?"

Emma just shook her head, exhausted. "Are you all right?" Joe asked worriedly, but she appeared not to have even heard him.

Suddenly Joe felt overwhelmed by the sheer hopelessness of their situation. He got up and quickly left the room. He didn't want Emma- or even worse, Dean- to see the tears brimming in his eyes.

Joe almost ran into the bathroom, slammed the door, and sat on the edge of the dusty bath. He glanced in disgust at the lines of dark yellow residue that crept from the tap and gathered around the plughole. *We're going to get caught,* he thought miserably as he wiped at his cheeks. *It's only a matter of time.*

He wished more than anything that Amber was with them. She probably couldn't have helped the situation, but just her being here would have made it better. *Where is she?* he wondered again. *What's happened to her? Why can't I sense her at all anymore? Has she... no, I can't let myself believe that...*

After a while he heard a knock on the door. "Joe? Can I come in?" Emma asked.

"If you want," he muttered.

She came in, closed the door quietly behind her and sat down next to him. "Not very comfortable in here," she commented with an uncertain smile. "Or very clean."

Joe shrugged tiredly.

"It feels like it's all too much, doesn't it?"

"It doesn't matter what it feels like," he replied. "We'll end up getting caught, and you'll go to jail and I'll end up in care and then the Order will *definitely* do whatever they want with me. That's why it was so *stupid* for the four of us to not stay together!"

"Joe, please let's not start this again. We haven't been caught, and I'll make sure that we won't be."

"You can't promise that!" Joe shouted. "There's too many of them. They're *everywhere!*"

Emma didn't say anything to that. Neither of them spoke for a while. Finally Emma said quietly, "Joe, you do know it wasn't your mum on the train, don't you?"

Joe looked at her, startled. "Of course I do!" He thought back to the words that had been spoken through the intercom on the train. "I'm falling forever," he said quietly. "That's what she... that's what *it* said. Would *she* have said something like that? I don't know."

Emma didn't say anything. Joe remembered the hole in the woods again. *Is she like the stones that Dean threw into the hole? Is it that easy for them to cast people into a kind of void, where they really do fall forever?*

"Do you think that maybe she *is* somewhere though?" he murmured.

"What do you mean, somewhere?"

"I... I'm not sure. A kind of limbo." A sudden, awful idea occurred to him. "What if she's trapped in the Emptiness?!"

"Joe, she can't be."

"How do you know?"

Emma put her arm around him. He glanced at her and saw suddenly how upset she was. "Because I watched her die," she said quietly. "I was with her when it happened. I was with her *and* your dad..."

"You were in the car with them?"

Joe saw a strange, fearful look in her eyes. "It... there wasn't a car crash. That wasn't what happened to them."

"But you always told me..." Joe shook his head in bewilderment. "Why would you lie to me about that?!"

"Because then you would have to deal with the truth, just as I have to every day." Emma looked steadily at him. "You weren't old enough for the truth, and I don't think I can tell you now."

"I'll deal with it," he said stubbornly.

"No. You won't deal with it, and I'm not strong enough to tell you anyway. All I can say for now is that they're both gone, and that's one of the few things that are certain in this world and every other. Believe me, I would give anything to have my sister back, but that's never going to happen."

"How...?" Joe felt his voice give way, and he tried to speak again. "I just don't understand. How could they have known what her voice was like? That *was* her voice, wasn't it? It felt like it was, even though I can't remember her properly."

"It was her voice, or a good likeness of it," Emma agreed quietly. "But it wasn't her. The Order are very good at working out people's weaknesses, the bad things that have happened in their lives. They can even use memories that they find inside your head. Memories that are deeply buried. That's what they tried to do on the train. They found something in a corner of your mind- something you probably didn't even consciously remember."

Joe bowed his head.

"They will do everything in their power to trick you," she continued. "But I won't let them win." She sounded as if *she* had started to cry now, but Joe didn't dare look.

They sat quietly together for a while. Finally Emma murmured, "You know, I was always jealous of her. My whole life."

Joe looked at her, startled. "You were jealous of my mum?"

Emma nodded. "She was three years older than me and I always thought I got treated unfairly, which is odd because they say the first born have it worse. I don't know." She took her glasses off and began to wipe absently at them. "And you know the silly thing? That jealousy carried on through adulthood. We loved each other, of course, but a lot of the time we really didn't like each other very much. And it got worse when... when I found out I couldn't have children."

"Oh." Joe looked uncomfortably at her. "I didn't know about that."

"No, well it's not something you tell a young child. You're old enough to tell now, not that it really matters anymore. But it gave me another reason to be jealous of her and your dad. The fact that they had *you*. That envy burned inside me right up to the day they were killed- and then of course it died with them. And a part of me died that day as well."

"I'm sorry," Joe said quietly.

"Some people say that time is a healer. I don't think that's true. Time just papers over the cracks in your life, and it doesn't always do it very well."

When Emma finally hugged him and got up to go, he looked up at her and his heart almost skipped a beat when he saw that her eyes looked different again. They were that same intense blue that he had seen on the train, filled with anger and sadness but somehow clear and strong. Joe found himself thinking suddenly of babies' eyes and how pure they appeared as they looked out into their new world. When he looked in the bathroom mirror before following her out, Joe was just as surprised to see that *his* eyes were now that same intense blue, just like hers.

I look determined, he thought, bewildered.

Why would I, when our situation is so hopeless?

"What are we?" he whispered as he looked back at himself. "What creatures are we, inside?"

Later that night, as he lay down and tried to get to sleep, Joe thought about the Emptiness and suddenly remembered something from the events of a year and a half ago. Some of the Lost had died *here* in this world before they reached the Emptiness. At least, that was what one of their leaders had told him. Was that true? Had they somehow been resurrected when they were pulled through into the Emptiness? How was that even possible?

He wondered if that meant that other people could die in this world but still be alive there.

I'm falling forever.

Those words echoed desolately in his mind as he finally drifted off to sleep and a swirl of unsettling dreams.

5

Morning came too soon for them all. Dean stared out of the window and watched the morning traffic that filled up the street below. He could also hear Emma writing some notes while she muttered quietly, and Joe showering in the bathroom. *If I closed my eyes I'd hear just ordinary sounds and could almost pretend nothing unusual was happening,* he thought. *I wish I could just send myself away to some other place, melt into the background and become normal, become someone from a different family, an ordinary family...*

Joe and Emma were anything but normal, he knew that. He liked them both, but something set them apart from everyone else he had ever known. The odd thing was that he felt as if they were similar to him in some way, as if they shared some deep, unspoken secret.

"Are you all right?"

He jumped and looked at Emma. He hadn't even realised that she was looking at him. "Um... yeah, I guess. Well no. Not really."

She grimaced. "Stupid question. Of course you're not all right. None of us are. We're on the run from an organisation which has infiltrated the world's societies like a slow-moving cancer. You must have so many questions."

Dean shrugged helplessly. "I wouldn't even know where to start."

"Anywhere you like."

He thought quickly. "When we first met and you held my hands for a moment... something weird happened. It felt like you used some power... I couldn't believe it at first but then I saw what you did when we were on the train, and I thought... did you read my thoughts?"

"Not exactly. I reached out to your subconscious, and I received a sort of... *snapshot* of your life. Like a condensed video. And it helped me work out why you were so desperate to come with us. But there was something more than that. Something I'd suspected but couldn't prove."

"What?" Dean asked guardedly.

"Your family are like ours, Dean. Your parents are both members of the Order, the same group from which Joe and I have been running and hiding for a long time now. My family- well, Joe's the only family I have left now- were once members of it too. Not part of the leadership or important in any way, at least not until Joe and Amber found their way into..." She smiled tiredly. "I'm beginning to realise just how much you don't know and how long it would take to tell you everything."

Dean didn't really understand, but he was too concerned about what Emma might have found out about him. "Can you promise you won't tell anyone? About why I had to come with you?"

Emma looked thoughtfully at him. "I'll do you a deal," she said finally. "I promise I won't tell anyone if *you* promise to not be ashamed of who you are. We're all different and we all have a unique place in the world. Don't be ashamed of yours."

Dean shifted uncomfortably. "I don't want to be, but you have no idea what my dad's like."

"Actually I do. In fact I now know almost as much about him as he does about me and Joe."

"Are you psychic, or a witch or something?"

"A *witch*?!" Emma laughed at that. "Not quite, although in older times I would probably have been burned as one. People feared knowledge back then. Many people still do. Religion and superstition have always hindered progress and rational thought. But I have certain powers, and so does Joe, although many of his haven't been unlocked yet. They will soon, I think. And you have your own. They burn quietly inside you."

"*Me?*" Dean blinked. "I don't have any powers. If I did I would have used them already and got away years ago."

"They don't really work like that, Dean. They're unpredictable, sometimes even dangerous, and they tend to stay dormant until you're older."

"So they could suddenly appear at any time?"

"They could." Emma paused and then said, "It's difficult to describe, but it's as if the life you had lived was just a dream. When the powers wake it's as if *you* wake, into a new reality. They're a part of who you are. I'll be honest with you‐ when it happened to me, it was frightening. I struggled for weeks‐ and I mean physically and mentally. There's nothing you can do but try to live with it. That's the brutal truth."

Dean jumped as Emma's phone rang suddenly. At the same time Joe emerged from the bathroom. "Who can that be?" he asked worriedly. "Who even *has* that number?"

Emma didn't say anything. She pressed the answer button and held the phone to her ear but she didn't speak. She listened intently to whoever had called and then hung up, without even saying goodbye to the caller.

The boys watched as Emma took the SIM out of the phone, put it to one side, and held the phone until faint tendrils of smoke emerged from it. Finally she crushed it in both hands and then threw the remains into the rubbish bin.

"What... what did you just do??" Dean asked faintly.

Emma didn't reply but placed her hand over the SIM on the table and pressed downwards. When she lifted her hand up the SIM was nothing more than a dark smear of dust which she blew away. "Wow," Dean whispered.

"I've seen her do that before," Joe murmured.

"Come on. It's time to go," Emma said briskly. "He's parked just three blocks away."

"Who is?" Joe asked.

"An old friend. The only one I have left who can be trusted."

The three of them made sure they had everything in their backpacks and then hurried downstairs. A different receptionist was on duty this morning. She was so busy texting someone that she didn't even bother to look up as they walked past and out of the front door.

It was still dark outside but a few lighter scraps of sky could be seen in the east. Emma, Joe and Dean made their way quickly down the road, and after a hundred yards or so Emma led them down a narrow, unlit side street. A car had been parked halfway down, and Joe saw a man in an overcoat and old-fashioned flat cap in the driving seat. He leaned across and opened the front passenger door when he saw them. Emma got in and motioned for the boys to get in the back.

"This is Tom," she said. "We need to stay with him for a short while. Tom, this is Joe and this is Dean."

"Hi," Joe said uncertainly.

"Good morning to you both," Tom said, as he started the car. He slowly drove out of the side street and onto the main road. "Bit of a mess, this, from what I understand," he remarked as they headed out of the town.

"It's Dean's fault," Joe said without thinking, and Emma turned round to give him a stare.

Dean turned and looked out of the window. Joe suddenly remembered how upset he had been last night and wished he hadn't said those words. "Sorry," he mumbled, but Dean had nothing to say to him. He pretended to be interested in the houses and street lights they passed.

Joe couldn't decide if Tom was worried or angry, or both. He looked like someone who hadn't slept in a while. Joe wondered if he had spent the last few weeks doing much the same as Emma, if he had constantly monitored current affairs or scanned Internet forums late into the night, making notes and gathering information, sorting through all the hatred and fake news.

What has Emma really been doing really? he wondered. *Has she planned for the end of the world all along?*

"It's happening, isn't it?" Tom said quietly as they waited at a red light. In the background a DJ on a local radio station cheerfully prattled away about something. Tom laughed for a moment, but he didn't sound happy. "I can't believe I just said that."

"Yes. It's happening." Joe thought that Emma's voice trembled slightly. "No going back now," she added lightly.

"Hmm. I often wondered if I'd see it in my lifetime," Tom commented.

"You will."

They soon left the town behind. Each road they turned off onto looked narrower and felt bumpier than the last. In a short while they were deep in the countryside and drove in the emerging light along narrow unmarked lanes bordered partly by tall hedgerows. Eventually the sun rose and bright golden rays spread across fields pale with frost. The cold and still countryside looked beautiful in the morning light. *It will still be beautiful when humanity is done with,* Joe thought.

After a while the road ahead widened a little and ended at a pair of ornate but rusty iron gates. Tom got out of the car and pushed the gates open. They screeched in protest against the surface of the road.

They drove on and around a bend in the road. A large, partly derelict manor house came into view.

Joe stared uneasily at the rambling old building, and the windows glared forbiddingly back at him as if the rooms behind them held dark secrets. The roof had tiles missing and tall, thin brick chimneys protruded from it, most of them partly broken. They looked as if they might crumble and hurtle to the ground at any point.

Even the bright morning sun did nothing to make the place look any less miserable. If anything it made the darkness behind the windows greater.

Tom parked the car around the back of the house, which lay in shadow. Joe shivered as they got out and followed him to a door which he unlocked. Early morning frost crunched quietly underfoot. "Is this where we'll be staying?" Joe asked doubtfully.

"Just for a few days," Emma said. "It wouldn't be safe to stay anywhere for longer. But hopefully we'll have enough time to decide what to do next."

They followed Tom into the gloomy corridor beyond. Their footsteps echoed harshly on the tiled floor.

The house had a slightly musty smell and looked a little worse for wear, but it wasn't quite as bad inside as Joe had feared it would be. "One of the drawing rooms on the first floor is in a better state. Might be a bit more comfortable," Tom said as he led them up a flight of stairs that creaked alarmingly under their combined weight. Joe placed his hand on the banister and it left a big smudge in the dust that had gathered.

They walked a short way down the landing beyond and then into a large, spacious room furnished with a table and chairs in the middle and antique armchairs in three of the corners.

"We've been on our own for a long time," Emma said as they sat at the table. "We have no friends or allies left. Only you, Tom."

Tom smiled uncertainly. "I'm not sure how much use I can be."

Emma thought for a while before she spoke up again. "I've watched the news almost constantly and spent time on the Internet doing research more than ever over the last few months. Actually the Internet is much more useful than the news channels if you look in the right places. Often the hours would slip by quickly, and I could feel time running out. But I wanted to be as certain as I could. Each clue led to several more, and slowly the evidence began to point to one specific, very simple plan. I used my powers to find out more..."

"Over the *Internet?*" Joe stared at her.

"In a manner of speaking, yes. It's not easy, it takes time and it often doesn't work. It's a bit like psychic detective work, with a lot of computer hacking thrown in, and..." Emma shook her head. "It doesn't matter. What *does* matter is that the world has fallen into chaos even more quickly, because the Order is not what we once thought. The Order and the Lost are more or less the same thing. Joe and I have known this for some time, Tom, but I guess you didn't."

Tom shook his head, clearly taken aback.

"As for their people- well, I suspect almost all of them have realised this by now, and those who dared to voice dissent or fought against what the Order has become, have simply disappeared, or unfortunate things have happened to them.

"Joe and I have been on the run for the last year and a half, because I found out that the Order planned to get rid of us. We kept ahead of them through sheer luck or their hasty tactics, but in fact we were hiding from one enemy. One organisation.

"Even back then I felt certain that they had been infiltrated, and *they* must have known that *we* knew. Joe and I- and a couple of friends of ours- were on the fringes of the Order really. Renegades, they would have called us‑ even back then."

"Amber and I found a way through to the Emptiness, Joe said. "After that they became a lot more interested in us."

"Who's Amber?" Dean asked.

"She's... she was..." Joe shook his head, unable to say any more about Amber. He turned to Emma. "There must have been some people in the Order who knew what was going on and could have told authorities and governments about them."

"No. No one would have believed them, and those who did would have pretended they didn't." Tom smiled grimly when Joe looked across at him. "I know enough about the Order to know that they've infiltrated the highest levels of government in pretty much every country. It's been going on for a long time."

"Centuries," Emma added.

Everyone fell silent for a short while, until Dean quietly asked, "So we hide here for a few days, and what then? We just keep running? Why? Our luck will run out eventually."

"There wouldn't be any point to that, of course," Emma agreed. "As you said, eventually we'd get caught. All we've done is buy a little time. I realise that."

Joe felt an unpleasant, creeping sensation as he heard those words. "You have a plan, don't you?" he said eventually.

"Not a plan exactly," Emma admitted. "But I don't think we have any choice. Wherever we go in this world, sooner or later they'll find us."

Wherever we go in this world. The words echoed through Joe's mind. "Oh no," he whispered as their true meaning dawned on him. "You can't mean..."

Emma looked afraid, but more determined than Joe had ever seen her. "We need to go into the Emptiness," she said. "But on our own terms."

6

Stunned silence filled the air. Joe had no idea what to say. He wondered for a moment if Emma had lost her mind. "No." He shook his head. "It's impossible. I can't go back there. I can't!"

"Joe, I don't think it will take them long to find us. Bad times are coming, but we have a way to escape if you can use your..."

"No!" he interrupted. "I don't even know if I *can* do it anymore. It only happened once, and I can't even remember how I did it. You told me not to even think about what happened, or don't you remember?"

"I remember," Emma admitted. "But things have changed."

"I didn't even know what I was doing. It was just... what's the word..."

"Instinctive," Dean said quietly.

"And I had Amber with me. I couldn't have done it without her, I'm certain. We were... I don't know, linked somehow."

"You were able to because our enemies were near," Emma told him. "And that's how you'll do it again. Your powers react to them like mine do- just differently."

"I'm not doing it. I can't do it."

"You will, Joe, because you won't have any choice. When they come for us, you'll know exactly what to do. Find a way through."

"Why can't *you* do it?" he answered back. "I've seen some of the things that you can do."

"I've never been able to open portals," Emma replied. "You may as well ask me to learn to fly. Our abilities are different, Joe."

Tom said quietly, "Emma, are you certain about this?"

"I'm certain that we have to try." She had never sounded so tired or so desperate. "I can't be certain about what will happen if we make it through. He's all I have left in the world, Tom, but he's the only way the four of us have of surviving what's about to come. I've thought about this for a long time and there really isn't any other way."

"And what if there's even more of them in the Emptiness?"

"I don't think there will be. They're gathering here. And we *all* know what will happen if we do what we've been doing for months."

Joe put his head in his hands. "I can't do it, Emma. I'm tired of all this. Let them do what they want. I don't want to run anymore."

"Maybe I can help," Dean spoke up.

"*You*?" Joe stared incredulously at him. "How?"

Emma turned to Dean. "Do you think you can?"

He nodded. "Maybe. I remember a few times when my dad threatened me I felt... I don't know, just something, like a rage inside me, but it wasn't just

110

anger, it was more than that. Mostly I would just be scared but there were a few times when I felt as if something amazing would happen if I just let go, let that rage wash over me and take me over. But I was always too frightened about what might happen, the punishment that I'd get. I knew that no matter what I did, he would be stronger than me and he would really hurt me afterwards."

"Did he hit you sometimes?" Joe asked.

"Yeah. A few times. Mostly he didn't need to. He's just a scary man. He's always been good at making people do what he wants without needing to get mad at them." Dean turned back to Emma. "So if others like him turn up, and I get that rage inside me, maybe that's how my powers will wake. Maybe *they* are just waiting for *me*. Waiting for me to let go."

Joe turned back to Emma. "Is that why you brought him along? You could tell he was like us? I suppose that makes sense if his dad's in the Order. I didn't think of that."

"Partly. Instinct had something to do with it as well."

Joe shook his head. "Well, even if Dean is able to help like Amber did, I can't say where we'll end up or even if anything will happen at all. I can hardly control it, so I doubt that you can, Dean. We shouldn't even be doing this."

"Maybe it's our only chance," Dean said.

Joe laughed bitterly at that. "I don't think we have any chance."

A short while later Emma nodded off and Tom went to prepare some food, although Joe couldn't help but wonder what sort of food left here might still be edible. Maybe he had some in his car. Dean said quietly to Joe, "So I guess she isn't really your mum, is she?"

"Emma's my aunt," Joe told him. "My mum's sister. My parents both died when I was much younger. I don't really remember them properly." He tried not to think about the voice on the train.

"Oh." Dean looked uncomfortable. "I'm sorry."

Joe shrugged. "People always say that to each other and it doesn't really mean anything."

"It means they're sorry."

"No. It just means they're embarrassed by something they said." Joe wandered restlessly over to the window. "I don't really want to talk about it."

Later that day Joe wandered around the house and found an old library on the ground floor, with a high, dark patterned ceiling and equally gloomy wood panelling around the walls. Bookcases crammed with dusty old books lined each of those walls and occupied almost every available space apart from where the door had been built. Like the rest of the house the library had a damp and musty smell. A wooden table had been placed in the middle of the room and a small pile of books had been left on it to gather dust. Joe wondered if any of them had been published in this century or even the last one.

Why would they just be left here to rot away like this? he wondered. *Maybe a large family lived here once but moved away. Does Tom own this place or is he just a warden for the estate?*

Out of boredom as much as curiosity Joe wandered over to the nearest bookcase. He reached out to take one of the books, wondering why it had no title on the spine. Then, as he pulled it from the bookcase he saw that it had no title or any other detail on either the front or back cover.

Joe frowned and stared at the book. The cover was made of leather, he thought, but there was something odd about the sensation against his skin.

For a moment he thought he could make out some faint letters on the front cover, but when he tried to look more closely they faded from sight.

He turned the book over again and idly traced a finger down the surface of the front cover, then suddenly pulled his finger away and almost dropped the book in shock. *I felt the cover move,* he thought, astonished. *It rippled and almost wrapped around my finger when I touched it.*

Hastily he put the book back in its place on the shelf and took a step backwards. *Something happened just then,* he thought fearfully. *Something important, but I've no idea what it was.*

Joe heard a faint shout from somewhere else in the house. A moment later he felt a prickly sensation wash over him, as if a million tiny creatures writhed underneath his skin. "Oh no," he whispered.

He quickly left the library and ran upstairs into one of the large rooms that faced the front of the house where he found Emma, Tom and Dean standing by the window.

Emma silently beckoned him over and gestured to the scene outside.

Joe walked over and looked out over the grounds and driveway, where at least fifty people stood, some on the driveway itself and others on the grass. What made the scene so unsettling was that these people looked entirely normal. They could have been picked at random from a crowd. Some wore jeans and coats, others wore suits. They were mostly men and women, of all sorts of ages and descriptions, but some were boys and girls. The oldest might have been over eighty and the youngest of them was probably no more than ten. A few shivered in the wintry breeze, obviously uncomfortable.

All these people were quite different to one another except for one thing.

Every one of them stared directly towards the window where the four companions stood.

A tall man with short grey hair walked slowly forwards. He wore a dark overcoat and his polished boots crunched loudly on the gravel of the driveway. Even from this distance Joe saw the coldly impassive look in his eyes and a stab of fear went through him.

"Good afternoon," the man said, and the companions flinched at how clear and *near* his voice sounded. "Or is it evening? It will get dark soon. I know that much."

Dean whispered something and then said in a small voice, "That's... that's my dad." He sounded full of hate yet frightened out of his wits.

"I don't expect you're interested in small talk, so I'll come straight to the point," the man continued. He sounded casual and utterly confident, as if he knew that sooner or later he would get whatever he wanted.

He put his hands in the pockets of his overcoat and smiled thinly. "I see you have my son with you. I'm afraid I'm going to need him back if you don't mind."

"Let me go," Dean said quietly, and turned to the others. "It's okay. Just let me go and he'll leave the rest of you alone..."

"That's right," his dad called out. "No one needs to get hurt, as the old cliché goes."

Joe's skin crawled and itched furiously as a ripple of power shimmered near the window. Dean's dad must have caused it. How else could he have heard what his son had just said?

"Oh- I haven't introduced myself," he continued. "I do apologise. My name is Alan Michaels. I just need Dean to come outside and then we'll go. As I'm feeling quite generous today I'll do you all a favour and conveniently forget to have you all charged with kidnapping and false imprisonment."

"Don't listen to him," Emma said to Dean. "You're not going anywhere."

Alan turned his icy stare to Emma. "Oh dear. Well, that's us off to a bad start. By the way, I know who *you* are."

"Likewise," Emma whispered.

Alan Michaels laughed, almost good-naturedly. "Yes, we've been watching each other for a while, haven't we? I had hoped to observe you for a while longer, but of course my son managed to... complicate matters. Dean is good at that."

Joe saw Dean shiver and cross his arms.

"This is silly," Alan remarked. "After all we're all the same deep down. You, me, all of us. The Free, the Order... they're just names, labels. The important thing is that there's *us,* and there's *them,* by which I mean everyone else- the millions of ignorant people that crawl around on the surface of this world like parasites. I don't suppose you've told Joe about that, have you? That we're the same? He does need to know, Emma. The boy should be allowed to make an informed decision. You *are* in favour of personal choice aren't you? Freedom of information?"

"What does he mean?" Joe asked. "We're not like them!"

"It's a matter of choice," Emma said quietly.

Joe's sense of unease grew, and the tiny prickles of power inside him and around him became stronger still. They felt like the crackles of electricity he sometimes felt when he put a jumper on, but far more powerful.

"Well, I wish we had a little more time to talk about all this, but we don't," Alan continued. "I get the distinct impression that you've chosen to ignore my offer." His voice remained calm but a hint of anger had entered it now. Joe wondered what he was like when he actually lost his temper, and decided he didn't want to know.

Joe looked across at Dean and found his gaze drawn to the boy's shadow, made by the light on the ceiling. *Something is happening,* he thought suddenly. *It's his dad doing it!*

The shadow began to move and change shape even though Dean remained still. Within a moment Dean had two identical shadows, one positioned where it ought to be based on the lighting and the other at right angles to it. Joe froze, horrified. *I should have told Emma when I saw it last time!* he thought frantically. *I didn't imagine it!*

Then Dean's other shadow became more solid and began to rise from the floor, a creature of absolute darkness shaped exactly like Dean. Joe heard himself shout in warning, just as the shadow creature reached out and began to envelop Dean in a black embrace. Dean's mouth opened in astonishment and then terror. He looked as if he was screaming, but no sound came from his mouth.

Even amidst this horror Joe heard Alan's voice, coldly distant yet clearer than ever. "This is what happens when you break the rules, Dean. I told you there'd be consequences if you disappointed me, and believe me you *have* been a disappointment."

Joe suddenly knew what he had to do. The idea filled him with fear but at the same time he realised he had no choice if he wanted to save Dean from this fate.

He stepped nearer to the other boy, and the strange forces that swirled around them all threatened to overcome him. *Stay in control,* a warning voice whispered in his head. *If you don't then everything will be lost.*

Do it now, he told himself, and he reached out and held both Dean and the shadow creature as tightly as possible, then let loose the shuddering power inside him.

It surged out of his body and throughout the room. Joe heard something that sounded like a flood of music, or joy in musical form. Then a howl of rage cut through it, and he knew instantly that the hatred and fear belonged to the shadow creature, a creation of the Order. In that same moment, he knew its nature.

Black and cold, this monster belonged only in the cold darkness of space. It came from a void where light never shone. The Order had created it using science far beyond anything Joe could understand. It had been pulled here and imprisoned, somehow attached to Dean and yet hidden most of the time. Joe knew all of this in a moment, as the shadow lashed out at him and tried to pull Dean away at the same time. *Mine,* it hissed inside his head, and the touch of that word felt like agonisingly hot smoke.

It existed to obey Dean's father, and even through the torrent of energy that now swirled around the room Joe felt Alan's initial surprise and then anger at his interference.

He concentrated on pouring all his energy, all the power that belonged to him and was part of him alone, into the shadow. It shook and raged against him, and finally it began to shrink, until the creature that had grown out of Dean's natural shadow disappeared entirely, consumed and crushed to nothing by Joe's power.

Joe swayed on his feet. The room swirled around him as if he had become trapped on a fast-moving carousel. He was vaguely aware of Dean trying to hold him up. *Your eyes,* he thought as he looked confusedly at the other boy. *They're like mine now. Like Emma's. Are you one of us? Did Emma know all along?*

"You've woken up," he heard himself mumble. "Welcome to the nightmare."

7

"Joe?"

He felt a hand gently shake his shoulder, and his eyes flickered open. He lay on a bed in one of the bedrooms. Emma sat on a chair nearby. Joe thought she looked haunted and about ten years older than just a couple of days ago. He wondered how much all this had taken out of her. He could see some streaks of grey in her hair. Had they been there before? He couldn't remember.

She squeezed his hand gently and forced a smile. "Are you okay?"

"I don't know. I feel... tired. Confused." The memory of the dreadful shadow creature suddenly swam back through Joe's thoughts. "Oh my god... what happened after I... I mean, where are Dean's father and the rest of them... did we, I mean, did you..." He tried to sit up and almost panicked when he found that he couldn't. All the strength had gone from his body. He collapsed back onto the bed. "It can't come back," he whispered, then looked at her. "Can it?"

"You destroyed it," Emma said soothingly. "And the Order have gone for now. I suspect Alan Michaels decided to retreat after his... creation was destroyed. He certainly didn't expect that, and may even feel that he underestimated us. But they'll be back with reinforcements. Maybe as many as they can recruit. It could be hundreds."

"Hundreds? Against us?" Joe uttered a weak laugh.

She nodded. "We can't hope to defeat so many of them. He'll want to make certain. That's why we have to leave and find a way through to the Emptiness as soon as you feel well enough."

Joe didn't want to think about that. "If they were supposed to be the secret keepers of world peace, then why have we had all these wars throughout history?"

"What purpose would they have in an entirely peaceful world?" Emma replied. "Every powerful organisation *needs* a certain amount of conflict, or else they struggle to justify their reason for existing. There are many groups that say their goal is to keep the peace. You know some of their names. But have you ever seen a peaceful world in your lifetime?"

"No," he admitted.

"No. Neither have I. And that's partly because it suits their agenda to have work to do. In any case, things tend towards chaos, and the more people try to hold onto power the more that chaos pushes against them."

Joe suddenly remembered something. "What did Dean's father mean? About us all being the same. We're not, are we? I mean, we're all part of the Order, or we *were,* but..." He stopped, no longer certain what we was trying to say.

Emma didn't reply for a while. Finally she said, "He's right in a sense. The difference is in how we all choose to use our powers. Making the right choices. That's *everything.*"

Emma stopped and thought for a moment. "You know that more and more atrocities are being committed everywhere across the world. Almost every day there's a massacre somewhere, a bomb blast somewhere else, riots in cities across the world, and a week can't seem to go by without a new faction having risen up against another one. It doesn't take much for whole countries to become completely lawless."

"People talked about it a lot at school," Joe remarked. "There was a lot of tension and fear."

"Everything's also become more unpredictable, and some of it is down to the sort of people the news channels tell you about. But not all. The Order work behind the scenes throughout the world. When you watch the news, it's difficult to tell the difference between the usual bloodshed fuelled by organised religion or racial tension, and events which are the direct work of the Order. They almost *are* the same thing, because their ultimate aim is a crazed dictatorship of the world with them at its centre. in control of everything. They're two poisons in the same water and they can't be separated."

"Why are they doing it?" Joe asked. "It doesn't make sense."

"Doesn't it?" Emma smiled sadly. "Once the world is brought to ruin they'll be able to step from the shadows and take over. They'll become the world government after all the nations have finally grown weary of tearing one another apart. And the unlucky people will be those who think they can survive by agreeing to serve the interests of their new masters. In fact, much of the Order's work can be done simply by encouraging humanity to wipe *itself* out. It's simply a question of how many corrupt governments, how many religious fanatics, how many squabbles over territory that the job requires. Meanwhile everyone else will see what's happening and start to panic. When people panic they lose sense and reason. They're even more likely to turn against each other. It won't take much paranoia and distorted information from the right organisations to do that. The Order will create rumours to stir up as much fear and hatred as possible on every network. Human nature will do the rest."

Emma took a deep breath and added quietly, "So, do you now see why we have to leave?"

Joe suddenly remembered an old T-shirt that Amber had owned a while back. On the front had been printed, "KEEP CALM, IT'S JUST THE END OF THE WORLD" in one of the many "Keep Calm" designs that had started to appear everywhere back then. He tried to recall when he had last seen her wear it, but couldn't. So many of his memories from that time had faded. He wanted desperately to remember the little details of that relatively ordinary life he had lived as a child. It seemed almost a perfect existence now, although it hadn't felt that way at the time.

I was lucky to have been content and happy and safe for so long, he thought. *No matter what happens now as the world closes in on us.*

Maybe *this* was the end of the world. If so, then it was nothing like how he had imagined it might be. No single thing had happened that would wipe everything out. No incurable virus, no plague of zombies, no meteor crash, no sudden breakdown of the world's weather. At least, none of those things had happened yet. It looked as if it would be slower and a lot messier than he had expected, and the people of the world would take an active part in their demise whether they knew it or not.

Joe couldn't think of anything to say for a while. He felt as if Emma reflected his own despair back at him. She had always been a solid, constant rock in his life but now she appeared desperate, unable to think of any plan other than running away to hide. He knew it was unfair, but he had hoped she would come up with an idea that involved them actually *winning*, rather than fleeing into the Emptiness- if they could even get there.

I guess I thought she could do anything, he thought. *Especially after I found out the truth about us. I looked up to her even more. But you can have miraculous powers and still be powerless. That's probably how she feels right now. It's how I feel.*

He sighed. "So we run and hide. What sort of life is that?"

"It's the only one left for us, Joe. These are desperate times." His aunt looked intently at him. "Are you well enough to get up if I help you? Tom has something he wants to tell us."

Joe sat up gingerly. "I think so."

They made their way through to one of the large living-rooms of the house, where Tom and Dean already waited for them.

"I doubt that we have much time," Emma said as she sat down. "Tom, do you want to begin?"

Tom nodded and cleared his throat. "Okay. I'll try to keep this brief. I know a fair bit about the history of the Order, and some years ago I stumbled across the legend of the Sleepers."

"I always thought they were a myth," Emma frowned. "Nobody alive today believes in them."

"You'd be surprised." Tom smiled faintly and continued, "The Sleepers were amongst the most powerful people in the ancient Order, which agreed that some of their people- the greatest amongst them- should be put into a deep sleep in a place protected from everyone and everything. Somewhere that no one could break into. This sleep would last forever if it needed to, or at least many centuries. As far as I understand the story, the Sleepers could be awakened in the event of unstoppable chaos. The end of the world, to coin a well-worn phrase.

"Anyway, my point is that perhaps now the Sleepers can be reached and awakened. Presumably the fortress that holds them can be breached if the world needs them to wake. Otherwise what point would there be in their existence?"

"If they exist at all," Emma pointed out.

"So they might be somewhere inside the Emptiness?" Joe said.

"They're just a story, Joe, as far as anyone knows," Emma reminded him.

Tom glanced at her and shrugged. "Perhaps, perhaps not. The little I can find on this whole matter suggests that they *might* be in a place within the Emptiness that the other people of the Order would be unable to breach..."

Joe felt the faint memory of the portal he and Amber had stepped through stir within him. *Were they trying to locate the Sleepers even back then?* he wondered. *Is that what the Order have been doing in the Emptiness all this time? Maybe the ones that called themselves the Lost weren't sent there or banished like they made out.*

Maybe they thought that the Sleepers could be a threat to their plans, so they hoped to destroy them before they could wake.

"But that's where the trail runs cold," Tom continued. "I haven't been able to discover anything more specific about their whereabouts. That's part of the problem with stories. They're all different to one another. The truth is often somewhere in between."

"But we only stand a chance if we can reach the Emptiness," Joe spoke up. "Is that what you're saying?"

"It's a very long shot regardless, Joe- but yes. Maybe together we can find clues that point to the location of the Sleepers." Tom sighed. "It sounds hopeless when I actually say those words. But if we're able to find a way through..."

"Even if we did find these Sleepers, how would we wake them up?" Dean asked.

"Some of the stories say that no one person can awaken them, no matter how powerful he or she may be. It would take at least two, possibly more, linked together. I was a little surprised that no one from the Order had documented this idea properly- I had to piece it together from the information I found. Perhaps the Order wanted to make sure the Sleepers could never wake, even back then."

"Do you think so?" Emma spoke up doubtfully.

"It's certainly possible. Maybe those amongst them who weren't already corrupt were tired of so many centuries spent trying to protect people from one another, only for terrible things to happen anyway. Of course, that just leads to the same fate for the world as the evil-doers amongst them hope for. Odd how every path seems to lead to the same place over time."

"What would happen if we *did* wake them?" Dean said thoughtfully.

"It's not going to happen." Joe had already heard enough about the Sleepers. "It's just a story."

"How would they put everything right?" Dean persisted. "Would they just find the Order and destroy them all, if they've become as corrupt as you say?"

"I don't know," Tom admitted. "They were meant to be the saviours of the world. But they were sent into their permanent sleep many centuries ago and meanings change over such a long time."

"Let's say they actually exist. What chance would we have of finding them?" Joe said. Before anyone could reply he continued, "*No* chance, that's what. Do you all really want to be trapped in the Emptiness forever?"

When no one responded to that either, he shouted, "I'm not going back there! I'd rather die!"

He walked away and left them standing in the silence of the drawing room.

8

The morning had dawned bright and frosty but as midday approached dark clouds began to mass.

"There's a storm on the way," Dean said as they gathered by the large south-facing window on the first floor.

"Your father will be back soon," Emma said as she wandered over to the window. "He'll bring more of them this time. Many more."

Dean laughed uncertainly. "You make it sound as if they're bringing the storm."

"They are." Emma turned to look at him. "It's almost inevitable when so many of them come together in one place."

"The cottage," Joe murmured as he recalled the storm that had howled around that house as he and Amber sheltered inside, alone apart from whatever it was that seeped through the ceiling.

Joe felt a violent shudder go through him suddenly. When he turned slightly he felt it change, as if a magnetic field worked its pull on him. He turned the other way and the feeling immediately lessened. After a moment he turned back and stepped forward in the direction where it had been strongest, and with every step he took the force gradually became stronger still.

Dean looked curiously at him. "What are you doing?"

"Something's calling to me. A... power of some sort," Joe said. "It grows stronger or weaker depending on which direction I walk in." He turned helplessly to Emma. "What should I do?"

"Go towards wherever it's strongest," she said automatically. "We'll come with you."

They followed Joe out of the room, down the corridor and down the stairs. Occasionally he stopped to check whether the strange pull had become stronger or weaker before he walked on again.

Eventually they reached the library, and it was here that Joe found that if he went towards either of the exits or the window, the pull lessened once more. But if he walked towards the bookcases it became so powerful that he could barely stop himself from rushing headlong towards the vast rows of books.

"It's somewhere here," he said breathlessly. "Hidden with all the books!"

Emma's expression was unreadable. Dean stared at him as if he had gone mad. Tom just smiled faintly and nodded as if he had expected him to say that.

Joe cautiously approached the bookcase and reached out his arm. As the strange, invisible current of power swirled around him he concentrated on the space between his outstretched hand and the rows of books. He thought for a moment that the air shimmered as if heat waves rose up in front of him, although he felt no change in the temperature.

Joe walked slowly alongside the bookcases and stopped abruptly when the pull began to fade again. He stepped back and touched one book after another until finally he found where the concentration of power was greatest. He carefully pulled it from the bookcase, and immediately saw it was the untitled book that he had picked up before. Again, when he looked at the cover he glimpsed some faint symbols, but they disappeared before he could point them out.

"Which book is that, Joe?" Tom asked quietly.

"The same one as before," he whispered, and suddenly feared that the odd rippling sensation would happen again. When he turned round, Tom gestured to the long table in the middle of the library. "Take it over there and place it on the table."

Joe went over to the table and put the book down. The others walked over, and Tom said, "Okay. Touch the cover again."

Joe did so, and three symbols appeared. They glowed faintly. One looked like a circle of light, the second a black circle with light all around the edge, and the third looked like an image of the Earth as viewed from space.

Totally entranced by the sight of these images, Joe moved his hand away from them and stepped back. To his amazement they began to rise slowly into the air, as if they were holograms projected from the surface of the book.

"Oh my god," he heard Dean murmur. "How cool is *that?*"

"What's happening?" Joe whispered, but no one had any answer.

Joe stared at each of the holographic images but he couldn't make sense of them. What did they mean? Did they mean anything at all? The image of the Earth was just that, he guessed. So did the ball of light represent the sun? And what about the disc of darkness?

"Maybe it's showing an eclipse," he said, but he didn't think that was the answer. An odd thought came to him. *Something has happened, but somewhere else.*

Joe turned to Tom, suddenly uneasy. "What was this book doing here in your library? You must have known about it."

Tom shook his head. "I have no idea about any of the books that were left here. I've never had time to read them."

Joe ignored him. "What does it do? And what's the book actually about?"

"I don't know. Why would I?" Tom stared back at him. "Didn't you open it to find out?"

"No. Because I knew there was something different about it. The cover felt like..."

Tom's gaze never wavered. "Like what?"

"Like... moving skin." Joe shook his head. "I know, it sounds ridiculous."

The images in front of them faded away, and at that precise moment they heard a low humming sound outside, almost electric. Joe felt his skin crawl and ripple, and when he looked at Emma he could tell that she felt the same way.

"They're back again." Joe began to walk over to the window and recoiled as a figure appeared and pressed against the glass. But it looked only at Dean, hard and intense eyes almost entirely red as if blood floated on their surfaces. Joe realised after a moment that this creature was Dean's father- now transformed into something that more closely resembled his true nature. The suave and icy police detective had been replaced by an animal in human form, filled with rage.

"*You had your chance, Dean.*" The words were uttered in a whisper and yet Joe heard them perfectly through the glass. Alan Michaels' voice hissed with fury. "You could have stopped all this. But you chose to stay here. You chose to *disobey* me!"

The window shattered abruptly and Dean's father sprang through the harsh explosion. A scream of hatred emerged from Dean's lips, and with it came a flash of pure illumination that dazzled everyone and made their view of the room nothing more than light and darkness. Alan was thrown back towards the broken glass, and a moment later a dozen other figures appeared at the window. *Destroy them,* whispered a voice in Joe's mind, as he saw Dean's arms outstretched towards the creatures that now swarmed over the broken glass.

Chaos erupted. Silhouetted figures swarmed through the light and were repelled by an almost invisible barrier that shimmered and distorted the companions' view. Joe heard screams and shouts and yet at the same time a voice whispered words in his head that he heard clearly. *This is our world now,* it told him, measured and cold, almost mechanical. *It was always destined to become ours. You creatures never change, weakened by your own greed and carelessness. Your great inventions and discoveries will amount to nothing in the fullness of time. Your nature will always bring you down sooner or later. And your time is now at an end.*

Events from the last few days and even the last year and a half swam through Joe's thoughts and filled him with fury. The trickery of the Order who had made his life a misery, using Dean to spy on him, or using the voice of his dead mother to try and weaken and confuse him, all the countless times he had felt afraid

133

in the last couple of years. These and many other images and feelings rushed through his mind and in only a moment they had built into a powerful, unstoppable force of rage.

Now the same light poured from him as well, but Joe barely noticed. Beings that might once have been human screamed in fear all around him, and yet they continued to their deaths, driven by desperation or compelled by their master.

As his rage subsided for a moment Joe heard himself shout for Emma, Dean and Tom to come closer to him. *I have to open up the way to the Emptiness,* he thought desperately. *There are far too many of them!*

He tried to remember how he had opened the way between the worlds before, but a sudden weakness almost overcame him, until he felt a hand grasp his and someone else's energy poured into him. Confused for a moment, he turned to see Dean. The boy looked like a reverse-contrast figure or someone in a negative of a photograph, his eyes dark pools in a face made from light.

"Let me help," he heard Dean say, but the words sounded inside his head. "I can do it!"

A moment later Joe felt the strangest sensation, as if he had become slightly displaced from the room they were in and had taken a step outside of reality.

Their surroundings began to change and fade, and the walls took on a bleak, ghostly grey appearance. Joe heard their enemies howl in desperation as if they had suddenly realised what Joe and Dean were trying to do. Joe held on tightly to Dean's hand, and almost staggered to his knees when a violent shudder of energy smashed against the barrier that Emma had created to protect them. Somewhere to his left it rippled and one of the creatures extended a dark arm towards them. Joe heard someone scream in agony and then the barrier shuddered back into place as Emma pushed back and the creature disappeared, swallowed up in white fire.

The room faded away entirely only seconds later. The harsh and hate-filled, desperate noise of their enemies dwindled to silence.

In a moment they had vanished from the world they knew.

Tom's eyes flickered open as a well-aimed kick to the ribs sent pain flaring through him.

He flinched when he saw Alan's cold eyes look dispassionately down at him as if he were an insect to be crushed under his boot.

"Get up," Alan said, and made his way over to the table across the room. Tom painfully got to his feet and followed, then sat down opposite him in the chair that Alan pointed to. All the creatures that had broken through into the manor house had disappeared, their work done for now. The only signs that they had been here at all were the shattered window and the broken glass strewn over the floor. Some of them had been destroyed, and yet no bodies remained as evidence.

The heat, Tom thought as he wiped at his forehead with a trembling hand. *So much energy was generated when Joe and Dean opened the gateway, and it still lingers here.*

Alan had placed the book on the table. With an idle smile on his lips he stroked the cover with one finger, up and down and then sideways to trace a cross shape. Tom watched him uneasily for a while. "Did it work?" he asked finally.

"Did Joe evoke the images when he opened it?" Alan rejoined.

"Yes." Tom described them, and Alan nodded, satisfied. "Then their journey should take them to where we want them to be. Joe was the one, as I suspected. And yet he needed Dean's help to open the gateway properly. No easy feat, doing that." Alan laughed unpleasantly. "Dean was useful for the first time in his miserable life."

Tom didn't say anything. He recalled briefly how the Order had first contacted him with their offer, weeks ago. He had been caught in two minds at first, hesitant about any betrayal of Emma but enticed by the promise of fifty thousand pounds. "Which you'll get to spend once things have settled down after we assume control," Alan had promised him.

And, he told himself, it had been a long time since he'd heard from Emma. He didn't mean anything to her. "She'll be in touch with you soon," Alan had said. "She doesn't have anyone else. That's all you are to her, Tom. A desperate last resort."

That fact had stirred anger within him, so Tom had betrayed her, and as time went on it felt more and more like the right decision. The world was changing rapidly. Alan called it a *realignment*. Old alliances and friendships would mean nothing. Nevertheless he had felt a pang of shame again when Emma duly contacted him, knowing that she had no one else left to turn to. But that had lasted only a short while. He fixed his thoughts on the money that would be his- not to mention a position of some authority in the new world government.

Oh, it's easy to betray your friends, he reminded himself as he watched Alan trace his finger along the book cover. *Everyone has a price.*

"Who wrote the book?" he asked curiously as he stared at the featureless cover.

"*Wrote* it?" Alan's smile was contemptuous. He opened it at a random page and flicked through. "It has no words, Tom. It's more a tool than a book- a very old one, passed carefully down over many centuries. I placed it here years ago. I knew that sooner or later the right person would find their way to it. All the time spent monitoring Joe and Emma was worth the effort after all."

Alan sat back in his seat. "I'm a man of subtlety, Tom. I knew that only the tiniest suggestion in the back of his mind would make Dean reveal to Joe that I had asked Dean to spy on him. Of course, I'd been doing it *myself* for months! And I knew that Joe would go running to his aunt. I mean, what else would he have done? These renegades are so predictable. That's why we've caught and dealt with almost all of them now. I even knew that Emma would know when contacts of hers *disappeared,* as we like to call it."

"I was the only one left," Tom said.

"You did well," Alan remarked. "Of course, it's a shame that you're not one of us."

"Not one of..." Tom blinked worriedly. Suddenly he saw movement to his left, and when he turned to look he realised with alarm that not all the creatures that had arrived with Alan Michaels had left. The two that made their way towards him appeared as if out of the shadows, disentangling themselves from the gloom. They looked almost human, except that their limbs were too long, their features too thin and pronounced, their tiny eyes too sunken back into their oversized heads. Wherever they walked, a concentration of darkness surrounded them. *How do they do that?* he wondered fearfully.

Tom tried to contain his panic. He turned back to Alan. "Look, I've done everything you asked of me..."

"You did. I have no complaints," Alan admitted.

"So why..." Tom shuddered as the nightmare creatures stood on either side of him and grabbed his arms. "Why punish me? You promised..."

"This isn't a punishment, and I promise a lot of things." Alan's eyes were like chips of ice as he surveyed his prey disinterestedly. "I just don't need you any more, Tom. Keeping you alive now your work is done would be a mistake." He smiled. "I do hope you understand."

Alan looked up his underlings. "Take him to one of the cellars, would you? I don't want a mess made in this room. I have work to do here and I quite like the view."

Tom found that he could no longer speak. His captors hauled him from his chair and dragged him away. After a while he closed his eyes, as if in desperate hope that he could wish himself away from this nightmare.

He feared that the two of them would torture him for hours before they finally disposed of him, but they didn't. His end came quickly, and Tom's last bitter thought before the blanket of darkness settled over him was not that he had been stupid or deceitful, but that he wasn't and could never be one of the Order. He was just like everyone else- a human worm crawling blindly through the mud of a failed world, desperate, miserable and about to die unremembered.

LUKE

"Can you hear me?"

Luke's eyes flickered open into darkness.

Cold rock lay underneath him. His whole body hurt. Wherever this might be, the savagely cold air was painful to breathe.

After a moment he managed to sit up, grimacing with pain, and realised that the darkness was not total. As he looked slowly around he saw that he sat on a ledge high up on a mountain, which overlooked a landscape of indistinct fields and valleys. When he looked up he saw stars wink into view, more with each passing second. *How is that possible?* he wondered.

Something shifted to his left and Luke flinched, suddenly remembering that someone had spoken to him. He was not alone, but he had no idea who or what his companion was, wrapped in a cloak and with their face shadowed by the brim of a wide hat. Shoulder-length hair gleamed a faint silver in the starlight.

"Ah. So you *are* awake." The figure moved and passed a bottle to him. Luke peered at its contents. "It's water," the man said, and tipped his hat upwards so that Luke saw his face for the first time.

"*Stephen*," he whispered, taken aback. "What... no, I mean..." He glanced into the night once again. "Where is this?" He tried to remember what had happened before he lost consciousness. *They found us,* he thought, horror almost overcoming him as he recalled everything. *We fought them and then everything went white, and I don't remember anything after that... Amber! Where is she?!*

"Where do you think this is?" Stephen replied.

Luke peered up into the heavens and nodded, dumbfounded. *The Emptiness,* he thought. "So this is it."

"Indeed."

"Amber opened it..." Luke murmured. "Maybe we both did... I don't know. I have to find her." He took a sip of the water. "Where is she?"

"I don't know. Somewhere here though, I'd guess, seeing as you are."

Luke tried to collect his thoughts. "Did you find your family?" he asked finally.

"They're dead." Stephen's tone was harsh and he looked away after speaking. "I found their graves," he added after a moment. "So my life suddenly became straightforward. I had nothing left in the world so I thought to myself, why live there? And I managed to open a path back to this place. It's amazing how much energy can be generated by sheer grief and despair, Luke- by setting fire to all the savagery inside yourself. But you already know that, or else you wouldn't be here. You and Amber opened the way, and you couldn't have done so unless your situation was desperate. That's one thing the Order still don't seem to have learned properly."

Luke stared into the starlit gloom for a while. "I should have been able to protect her," he said finally. "That's the first duty of a father."

"You can't always protect those you love against the ways of the world and those who infect it," Stephen pointed out quietly. "I should know."

Luke got unsteadily to his feet. "I have to find her." He looked at Stephen again. "How is that *you* of all people found me?"

"Pure luck. I saw the light of your arrival from down in the valley over there." Stephen pointed into the gloom. "A sudden glow, just for a moment. I didn't know it was you, but I *did* know it wouldn't be one of our enemies. So I went to find out. I found you here, unconscious."

"How long have you been here?"

"I honestly couldn't say. Time is more fluid in the Emptiness, Luke. I don't think about it. It's not as if I'm going back. Remember, I have nothing to go back to, and in time it will become safer here anyway. The Order's followers have been steadily leaving this place. Preparing for the end of times." Stephen shrugged. "Which makes it easier for me to explore."

"Is that all you care about now?"

Stephen looked surprised. "Yes. Why would it be any other way?"

Luke shook his head. "Never mind. How do I find her?" He surveyed the shadowy landscape that stretched away below them. "How large is this place?"

"Wider and deeper than you could imagine. But don't lose hope. The link the two of you share is more powerful here. Head towards the centre."

Luke frowned. "You're not making sense. Where *is* the centre?"

"Head down there, to the wide valley. Stand still on the path for a short while, and you'll know which direction to head in from there on. Sooner or later, you'll find your way towards the centre. Our families were outsiders in the Order, Luke. Different, somehow, in ways that remain a mystery to me. That's why the Emptiness treats us differently. It leads us by the hand without our knowing. The Emptiness is the one thing we can truly have faith in."

"You make it sound like a living creature," Luke said.

Stephen just smiled at that.

Luke began to walk away. "Are you coming?" he asked when Stephen didn't move.

The other man shook his head. "No. Not yet, anyway. I hope you find her."

"Is it always night time here?"

Stephen laughed. "Luke, if you spend long enough in this world, and you might, then you'll see how it isn't night at all."

AMBER

1

Amber's eyes flickered open and the cobwebs of sleep swiftly fell away as she sat up in a sudden panic.

She had fallen asleep with her back against the wall of a building near a crossroads. The many signs and traffic lights indicated that in the world she knew, this area would be busy with traffic and probably gridlocked. But here, absolute silence reigned.

Amber shivered, struggled to her feet and put her hood up over her head. After a moment she made her way over to the nearest junction and looked at a few of the signs that showed directions to other parts of the city. She felt as if she ought to be able to read them but for some reason she couldn't, as if they became blurred when she tried to study them.

After a while she gave up and tried to work out which direction she ought to take. She still hadn't decided when she heard a car approach in the distance. Judging by the sound it made, it was moving quickly. Amber swiftly darted behind an old phone box as the noise grew louder. By the time the car went past along the road that criss-crossed hers, Amber had against her better judgement peered around the side of the phone box. Although she caught only a fleeting glimpse of the people in the car, she felt certain that one of them turned its head towards her for a moment.

It had no face, Amber thought in mute shock as the harsh sound of the vehicle faded into absolute silence. *Just smooth skin with no features. Nothing else.*

So why do I feel as if it saw me or somehow knew I was here?

She tried to swallow down her fear and gazed up into the sky where thousands of stars glittered. *It's as if I'm looking out from the middle of the galaxy,* she thought suddenly, and then wondered why she would think that or how she could know such a thing. *Is that where the Emptiness is? The middle of the galaxy? The stars didn't look like this last time. Or did they? I can't remember.*

Amber decided to put unsolvable questions to one side. Finding a way back was far more important. She suddenly wondered how long she had spent here, and that thought led onto another. *I ought to be hungry by now,* she thought. *But I'm not. What if there's no food here? Will I just starve? Or will I never need to eat? Surely I'll need to drink water?*

A sudden memory blossomed in Amber's head. *The house in that abandoned village,* she thought. *Joe and I went into it and then the old woman saw us leave afterwards... but she wasn't human at all. And then we met Stephen.*

Is he still here somewhere, or did he become lost in the void when we stepped through the gateway?

I need to find Dad, she thought. *But I haven't a clue how I'm going to do that. He must still be alive. I'd know if he wasn't!*

She cautiously began to walk along the pavement, but then something tall, pale and painfully thin stepped from the shadows just ahead. It gleamed like porcelain in the starlight. Amber stopped and stared at it, horrified. The creature had no mouth, nose or ears that she could see, only two wide, dark eyes that looked like big pools of ink. Its arms ended in long, almost needle-like claws. It wore no clothes but she couldn't tell if it was male or female- it didn't look like either. It crouched down as it wandered into the road, then turned slowly to look at her. One arm reached up and made a motion as if it wanted her to come nearer.

"I don't think so," Amber whispered, and she took a step back. Then, as it moved slowly towards her she raised her arm as if to defend herself, although she had no idea what to do. No force stirred inside her this time, and yet the creature stopped. Amber thought she could see fear in its eyes for a moment, but then realised that nothing could be seen in those eyes except a distorted reflection of the city roads and buildings. *Maybe it won't come any closer,* she hoped.

But she was proved wrong. Fearful it might have been, but something drove the creature to run at her suddenly. Amber's powers woke immediately in response, and she recalled what she had managed to do in the library. She stretched out her hand towards her enemy, and a flash of light suddenly cut through the darkness to strike the creature. Amber had expected it to cut straight through it, but instead the light reflected off its body. As Amber shielded her eyes, her enemy howled in pain and shock, turned and scuttled back through the shadows. Within a moment it had vanished.

Amber's knees trembled and she reached out her hand to support herself against the wall of the nearby building. A cold sweat began to break out on her forehead and under her eyes. For a moment she felt certain she was going to be sick.

There are worse monsters than that, a voice in her head whispered. *Those that look like people are worse, because they work their way into other people's lives, so they become trusted, even loved.*

She wondered if the Emptiness stripped all pretences away so that the truth revealed itself. Could it somehow be like a reflection of her world?

More memories came back to her, of Andrew and Helen in the prison where she had been held. *They looked human, but they had no humanity,* Amber recalled. *When I imagine their faces now, it's as if nothing at all existed behind them, like their eyes were just painted on, the faces were just a front and if I scratched them away I'd see nothing at all beneath. Just empty dark space.*

Amber wondered how such awful thoughts came so easily to her these days. Was it simply part of growing up and her futile attempts to make sense of a world that even adults struggled to understand?

She crossed at the junction after listening carefully in case any more cars approached, then headed along the road opposite. The starlight had grown so strong that she could see by it relatively easily, but after about two hundred yards one of the unlit streetlights suddenly flared into life. Its white brilliance appeared far greater and harsher than it ought, so that it lit the street for more than a hundred yards in both directions.

Amber suddenly realised something.

That light is the exact same colour as the light that comes out of me when I set my powers loose.

She had no idea how she could possibly know such a thing. After all, wasn't light just light? But she felt certain it was identical, that the strange energy within her and contained inside the streetlight were one and the same.

Tentatively Amber stepped nearer and realised that the light provided not only illumination but also a strange, comforting warmth. She stopped directly under the lamp post and felt her powers stir and ripple slowly as if in response to the white brilliance in which she was bathed. *It's a pulse,* she realised after a moment, bewildered by her discovery. *It's like the pulse of my blood, but in response to the light.*

A narrow alleyway led away from the pavement near to where the lamp post stood. Amber peered down it and saw that the light extended about twenty yards and then ended abruptly rather than fading away.

That's where I need to go, she decided, as if the pulse of light had silently told her.

Amber began to walk down the alleyway but stopped as she reached the edge of the light's reach, uneasy. Eventually she walked further on and found that the starlight remained powerful enough to illuminate the way ahead. When Amber stopped to look up she saw that even more stars now lit up the portion of visible sky above her, framed by the buildings on either side of where she stood. *How is that possible?* she wondered. *How can more stars appear just like that? There are no clouds in the sky but there weren't earlier either.*

The alleyway eventually stopped at a doorway set into a brick wall that stood so high she could barely see the top of it. The bricks appeared to simply converge and disappear into the sky. She noticed that beyond the doorway a flight of steps led down.

This can't possibly be a way out, Amber thought as she peered doubtfully at the stone staircase. *It doesn't look right. Why would there be a doorway and steps here at the end of an alleyway?*

But despite that she remained certain that down the steps was the best way to go, even if it didn't lead directly out. Maybe she had to go further into the Emptiness to find an exit from it. The idea made a strange kind of sense. *Isn't that what we did last time?* she thought, as a memory of underground caverns loomed in her mind.

Amber made her way down the first few steps and noticed that the staircase began to spiral. A soft yellow light glowed above as if the entire ceiling was a light source.

She took another few steps down. At the same time she kept one hand on the centre of the stairwell and tried to steady herself.

After some time Amber arrived at a doorway that led into a large, empty and unfurnished room. More open doorways stood in each of the walls, and when she crossed to peer through each of them Amber found that short passageways led through into other rooms. The ceiling of each room was lit by the same yellow glow that had illuminated the staircase.

Everywhere is open, Amber noted. *As if I'm expected. Maybe I should be afraid.*

She wandered until eventually she found a room where a door stood in place of one of the doorways. Made of shiny metal and studded with rivets, it looked like the door to a bank vault, but as Amber approached she felt certain that she had to pass beyond this door somehow. *Why else would it be different?* she asked herself.

When she touched the cold metal surface a barely audible click sounded from somewhere within. Hardly able to believe that something had happened just because she touched the door, Amber pushed tentatively at it, then again more forcefully when it refused to budge. This time it swung slowly open to reveal a passageway beyond.

Lit by harsh electric lights, this area glistened like a hospital corridor and stretched so far into the distance that the walls, ceiling and floor appeared to merge together. Amber wondered how and why anyone would have built a system of underground rooms and passageways as vast as this.

As Amber walked down the corridor, strange, frightening sounds came from behind the doors that she passed. But despite her fear she still couldn't help but stop and listen to them.

Voices, she realised after a moment.

Some were low and muffled, others shrill and clear. All of them sounded as if they belonged to people who were either being tortured or carrying out that torture. Some didn't sound at all human. The noise filled with her with horror. She tried not to imagine the scenes that were being played out in these hidden rooms.

Fearful that she would make too much noise herself and attract attention if she ran, Amber opted for a fast but steady walk. Luckily her shoes made almost no sound on the floor and nobody opened any of the doors. Noise that might have been made by machines of some kind came from behind some of them as she walked past a little later. She looked back a few times and imagined the lights in the ceiling being switched off loudly one at a time like she'd seen in a few horror films that she'd watched at a friend's house years ago.

Stop it, Amber told herself fiercely.

She fixed her attention on a door that she now saw at the far end of the passageway. As Amber drew close she saw that the door had a keypad and something that looked like it might be a retinal scanner, although she couldn't be sure.

The door was closed, but as she came within several paces a click sounded, and the door opened a few inches as if her approach had somehow unlocked it.

That shouldn't happen, Amber thought immediately. *It's too convenient. I should get out of here.*

She stood still for a moment and wondered if her next few steps might lead straight into a trap.

But the same strange urge that had taken her this far finally convinced her to step forward and open the door a little further just to see whatever lay on the other side.

At first Amber saw only faint light when she peered past the doorway. Then, almost before she realised it she had stepped through, and soft lighting came on soundlessly in the room beyond.

Amber's mouth opened in mute shock. She didn't even hear the door close and click shut behind her.

Throughout this huge room, bodies stood trapped inside glass pods embedded in the walls, held up in their clear prisons, arms at their sides, their eyes closed.

2

"Who are they?" she whispered eventually. "Why are they here?"

Amber shook her head, unable to believe that she had found her way to this place, that the door had opened for her and that these people were on display here, as if someone had intended for her to see them.

Maybe they did, came a whisper in her mind.

Amber walked slowly up to one of them. She looked at the woman's smooth features and wondered how old she might be, and how long they had all been trapped here. *They could be hundreds of years old,* she thought suddenly, and found herself reminded of a science fiction book she had read a crew kept alive in pods inside a spaceship. They had been asleep for over a century.

Who put these people here? she wondered suddenly. *This must have happened for a reason. Are they in some kind of really deep sleep?*

Or are they just dead?

That unpleasant possibility hadn't occurred to Amber before now. But when she cautiously walked nearer to some of them again saw their chests faintly rise and fall again as they breathed. Thick wires entered their backs in four separate places, and an extra thick cable had been attached to the backs of their heads. Why would anyone do *that* if it wasn't to keep these people alive for some reason?

Were they even human? They *looked* human, but...

The stars are different here, Amber reminded herself. *And they also look different to when Joe and I found ourselves in the Emptiness before. What if the Emptiness is not just one world? What if it's a collection of alien worlds?*

Her head began to hurt as she grappled with that idea.

Amber felt a strange thing happen as she once again recalled her previous time in the Emptiness. All of it came steadily back to her in vivid, exact detail as if an ever-present fog cleared from her mind. In a matter of moments she had remembered everything, and immediately wished she could forget all of it.

Then she realised that something had changed.

When she turned and looked around, she saw nothing obviously different, but she still had the creepy sensation that all the people in the pods were somehow aware of her presence, even though none of them had opened their eyes or moved.

Then she heard words whisper in her mind, clear and commanding.

Help us before it's too late.

Help us wake and stop the disease.

But Amber felt too frightened to listen properly. She was simply petrified at the fact those words had been uttered, that these people had tried to communicate with her, even in their sleep.

She turned and ran headlong through one of the many exits from the hall and down a gloomy passageway where only half the lights worked. When she arrived at a junction she picked a new direction at random, too panicked to slow down or make any reasoned choice.

Amber continued until she couldn't run any further. Exhausted, she sank down to the dusty floor, closed her eyes and wished that she could simply take herself away from this labyrinth by sheer force of will.

But she couldn't, and when she opened her eyes she saw long corridors that stretched away from her, paths that led only to other paths. For a moment she heard a faint rumbling, grinding sound, as if vast but distant machinery had been turned on.

I'm lost in Hell, she thought. *I'm lost in Hell and I'm going mad.*

Amber got up eventually and began to walk again, but she felt curiously empty. All her energy had departed and she had no purpose left, nowhere to go and nothing to hope for. *I've only become more lost,* she thought miserably. *Is that what happened to those people trapped in the pods? Were they just travellers in the Emptiness, captured and put to sleep? Why?*

Amber was about to sit and rest again, no longer certain that she would be able to get up afterwards, when she suddenly realised that she was being followed.

The swarm of creatures came for her quickly, perhaps aware of her powers and desperate to make certain that she didn't stand a chance. Amber couldn't muster a spark of resistance. *I'm done,* she thought as her enemies held her down. A bag was thrown over her head and rope tied around her wrists and ankles. *I'm finished, and it's probably about time.*

JOE

Joe opened his eyes to a night sky.

The darkness appeared alive with points of light. Stars glittered everywhere. *No moon,* was the first thought that came to him. *There's never a moon here.*

That thought crystallised in his head as he sat up. *I did it,* he realised, dumfounded. *I don't know how, but I did it. I brought us here.*

He saw movement from the corner of his eye and noticed that both Dean and Emma had sat up. *Dean helped me when I needed it,* Joe recalled. *We wouldn't be here without him. We would have been torn to pieces.*

His eyes adjusted quickly to the gloom. A fully moonlit night could not have been much brighter. As their surroundings came into view, he saw that they were in the centre of a vast, partly-ruined old building. The roof had caved in long ago to leave the place open to the sky, and so had parts of the walls. Wherever the walls had caved in, and in cracks and holes across the ancient stone floor, plants sprouted and crawled their way through the structure, as if they were eager to make this place their own.

"Is everyone all right?" he heard Emma say, followed by "Oh..."

Joe looked around. "Tom's not here."

"They must have got him," she said quietly.

Joe nodded. He wanted to say that he was sorry but knew it wouldn't help. He wondered how close his aunt had been to Tom and resolved not to ask. It wasn't any of his business, and it was too late now. He thought back to that moment before the Order returned. There was something about the way Tom had looked at him...

It doesn't matter, Joe told himself. *Tom's gone, and we're here. We may even be here forever.*

The three of them sat for a while longer and silently observed their new environment. "Thanks for helping me," Joe said to Dean eventually.

The boy looked caught in a spell as he stared speechlessly around. "Is this it? The Emptiness?" he murmured eventually. "Look at all these stars. I can't believe there's so many..." He laughed uncertainly. "This is crazy. I keep thinking this is a mad dream and I'll wake up, and then things get even crazier." His expression changed quickly. "I'd rather not. I don't have a lot to wake up to."

Joe studied the night sky again. "It's not like it was before. Maybe we're in a different area. I don't know why there are so many stars. It could be..." He frowned, suddenly aware of the idea he had stumbled on. "It could be that this is a different world. But still the Emptiness. I don't know."

"You mean it could be spread over many different worlds?"

"It's entirely possible," Emma said without turning round. "One world that touches many others. Yes, there are stories and theories..." Her voice drifted away and she looked around in silence. Joe wondered what she was thinking. Maybe, like Dean, she could barely believe that they had escaped their enemies and found their way here. He could barely believe it himself.

Joe got to his feet, and it was then that he suddenly felt Amber's presence again. The sensation of her return was so strong and filled him with such belief that he almost cried out.

She's alive! She's here! he told himself as his heart raced. He looked wildly around is he expected her to step out from behind one of the half-fallen stone walls. *Maybe I can find her somehow. How far away is she? Which direction?*

"It's Amber!" he blurted out, unable to stop himself. When the others looked at him he made an effort to calm down and continued, "Amber is somewhere here, I mean in this world. I'm certain of it!"

"How can you be?" Dean asked.

"It's difficult to explain. I mean, it's... no, it's impossible. I'd lost my connection to her, but now..." Joe felt oddly frustrated when he thought about the matter a bit more. Amber surely wouldn't have come back here of her own free will. Could she and Luke have opened a way back to the Emptiness? Why would they have done that? No, something must have happened to her, just as he'd suspected- and now he had to find her.

He thought back to that moment days ago, when that sudden dreadful knowledge that she was in great danger had descended on him. He had never felt worse than in that precise moment, overwhelmed by the certainty that something terrible had happened and unable to do anything about it. Could that have been the moment when she opened a way through into the Emptiness?

"We have to find her," he said firmly.

"Can you tell if Luke's here as well?" Emma asked tentatively.

Joe shook his head. "No. I mean, he might be, I guess... I don't know. It only works with Amber. I don't know why." He turned in each direction and tried to work out whether going that way would take him nearer to Amber or further away. Finally he decided to head across the castle floor towards an area of rubble where the walls had fallen away entirely. The remains of the stonework gleamed faintly in the starlight.

"How far away is she?" Dean asked.

"I don't know. I can only tell if I'm getting nearer to her or further away." Joe turned to look impatiently back at them. "Come on!"

The companions clambered over the rubble of the wall and made their way out into open grassland that stretched away under the bright starlight and sloped down into a valley. When they walked around in a circle they realised that the ruins stood on a steep hill surrounded by thick forest on all sides. The woodland stretched away for as far as they could see into the distance.

Dean groaned. "It goes on for hundreds of miles!"

"Maybe. Maybe not." Joe recalled the journey that he and Amber had made with Stephen a year and a half ago, into the catacombs where the gateway was located. He remembered that they had somehow covered a great distance more quickly than ought to have been possible. *I hope that rule applies everywhere here,* he thought as his weary gaze took in the many miles of thick woodland.

"This way," he said finally, and set off down the grassy slope. As the others walked on either side, Dean asked, "So, this girl... Amber? Is she your... you know..."

Joe hastily cut across him. "She was my best friend. I haven't seen her for a long time." He glanced at Emma. "We had to go our separate ways."

"So the Order are after her as well?"

Joe nodded. He didn't really want to say any more or think about what might have happened to Amber. He was desperate to find her as quickly as possible.

They reached the bottom of the hill. A narrow path led into the woods nearby, the way ahead lit by odd-looking lanterns. Some of them hung from the trees, while others had been placed on sticks to create makeshift lamp posts. *There were lights like this before,* Joe thought as they reached the tree line. *Is this the same forest? But how can this even be the same world if the stars look so different?*

He wondered suddenly if this might be a different hemisphere of the same world. He remembered learning that the stars in Earth's northern and southern hemispheres were different because the people in the two hemispheres saw different parts of the night sky. Maybe one hemisphere looked outwards from the galaxy and the other one- this one- looked directly towards its centre.

But this is the same forest, he thought. *Does it stretch across the whole world?*

"Are they all battery powered?" Dean asked as he peered at a couple of the nearest lights. Carefully he picked one of them up. "No, they're not. How do these lights get their power? Solar, do you think? Who put them here?" He looked further down the path and into the gloom. "I don't think we ought to go into the woods."

"In case you forgot, the forest is all around us," Joe reminded him. "We just need to stay on the path."

"How do you know that?" Dean shivered. "You make it sound like a creepy fairy tale."

"Where do you think the path leads, Joe?" Emma asked.

Joe thought for a while until the answer came to him. He was absolutely certain of it, just as he now knew that *all* the paths into the forest led to that same place.

"The cottage," he said. "It *always* leads to the cottage. That's where the centre is."

Another memory came sharply into focus, but this one didn't belong to him. He looked out from the window of the bedroom in Stephen's cottage, where he and Amber had slept for a night. Stephen stood outside and faced a creature of the Order- a thin-as-sticks woman whose eyes were full of cunning.

That's Amber's memory, he thought, scarcely able to believe it. *She must have watched as Stephen stood up to that creature, to protect us while we stayed at the cottage. Even though he betrayed us later on. But I suppose that was just because he needed us. He needed me, anyway- because he knew about the portal that the Order were working on, and he knew he could only get home if he went with us through the portal. He already knew that even though I didn't at the time.*

He saved us and then he used us.

Something about the cottage and possibly the whole woodland made it a place of power within the

Emptiness. Joe tried to grapple with the thought of distance being different, a world like a flat circle with the forest at its centre, or perhaps like a whirlpool, again with the cottage right at the very centre where things could fall through to some other place. Maybe even a deeper part of the same world.

Might that be why it was quicker to get anywhere by going through the woods, rather than around them, if that was even possible?

Joe pressed on into the woodland and the others hurried after him.

The noises of this forest were almost familiar but somehow eerily different to how they ought to sound. Occasionally a great sigh like a gust of wind could be heard far above them, and yet the leaves of the trees didn't rustle. They heard faint whispers and whistles as if unknown creatures called softly to one another through the endless night. When they passed through clearings and the path lay open to the sky, the starlight gleamed more fiercely than ever and Joe wondered if the sky would be ablaze with cosmic light when they finally reached their destination.

"I think I'd like to stay here," Dean said quietly as they rested a while later. "I feel like I'm... stepping out of the dark. My life was awful. I was afraid all the time. Now, I don't feel scared even though I probably should. Does that make sense?"

Joe and Emma exchanged glances. Neither of them knew what to say, but Dean was too wrapped in his thoughts to notice. "It's peaceful here and everything is a mystery. Where we came from, mystery was dead. And I feel... peaceful inside, somehow."

Joe didn't voice his fear that they might be stranded here forever.

As they walked on, Joe had the strange feeling that they had started to cover the ground more quickly even though their pace hadn't changed as far as he could tell. *It pulls us closer and the pull grows stronger,* he realised. When he looked in the direction that the path took them, a spiral that wound deeper into the forest, he could feel that invisible force, like a strange form of magnetism.

The companions walked until finally they turned a corner and the cottage stood no more than fifty yards away in front of them.

The strange pull became so strong as they approached the door that they could barely stop themselves from running straight at the building. They all heard a sound in their heads like the rush of a waterfall. The noise reminded Joe suddenly of when he had walked under a waterfall with the Guardian. Even that felt like a lifetime ago now. *It's as if the past is rushing back to greet me,* he realised. *The pull of this world, the sigh of the wind, the roar of the waterfall... this is the place where it all comes together.*

Joe reached the door first and touched the handle. At that exact moment both the pull and the noise stopped abruptly, as if the act had somehow broken a spell. The murmur of strange, otherworldly creatures that lurked in the unknown swathes of woodland all around also ceased, as if they now expected something to happen.

Stephen used a key when we were here before, Joe recalled. *But I don't think I'll need one. This time the house will let me in.*

Did he know what the house actually is? Maybe he was somehow trapped there. Maybe he had to go back every night. It would have been the only safe place for him.

"Are you sure about this?" Emma whispered, interrupting Joe's tangled train of thought.

Joe nodded. "This is the way through." He couldn't be entirely sure what he meant by that, but as he turned the door handle and the door opened to reveal the hallway beyond, Joe knew what to expect.

Beyond the hallway another door lay partly open. The companions could see shadows and light that danced on the walls as if from a fire that burned fiercely somewhere in the room.

When they stepped through, the light became stronger and they saw a doorway at the other side of the room. The illumination in the room made the darkness beyond the exit appear even blacker, almost like a live creature that could reach out and eat its surroundings.

"What is this place?" Emma murmured.

"I came here last time," Joe said. "But that doorway wasn't there. It's changed."

Dean looked at him. "Where do you think it leads?"

"I can't be certain. But I know we need to go through it."

As they walked up to the doorway they saw steps leading down. "It's as if... this way opened just for us," Emma said. "Why would it do that? I don't think..."

But Joe had already stepped through into the dark.

AMBER

1

Amber grimaced as she was forced down roughly onto a chair. Someone pulled the bag from her head, and she blinked and looked around the dimly-lit room. She had been seated at a long table, above which a single light bulb hung.

She looked warily around at the six others who were seated at the table, and a tremor of fear went through her. She recognised a few of them. Andrew, the man who had talked Joe into opening the gateway. Arik, the frightening creature who had taunted her as she lay imprisoned in a cell within the Emptiness a year and a half ago. That memory, suddenly so sharp in her head, was almost unbearable.

A man dressed in a suit gazed steadily at her. Amber didn't recognise him, but the way he looked at her made her skin crawl. She folded her arms and looked determinedly away from him.

"Hello, Amber." Andrew sat at the other end of the table, his lean and angular face full of hard lines and shadows. "I'm so glad to catch up with you again. We've heard a lot about your recent escapades. We *had* thought you might have disappeared forever. But everything comes to those who wait. We know that better than anyone."

Amber didn't answer. Her mouth felt completely dry and she was so frightened that she couldn't even think. The ceiling and the edges of the room were beyond her view, and the darkness gave the uncomfortable illusion that this place might somehow go on forever or at least far beyond any normal dimensions.

Arik leaned forward. Even though he sat some distance away, he appeared to loom over her. "If I had it my way, you'd be punished for what you and Joe did," he whispered. "Perhaps you already know where some of us ended up after he *amended* the portal? Antarctica."

Amber couldn't help but smile at that, but her smile vanished when Arik continued in a low hiss, "A minor inconvenience. Those of us who stepped through the portal and survived managed to find a way out on a science ship after a few months."

"Really?" Amber's fear had left her for a moment. "*You* left on a ship and it wasn't reported?"

"Oh, I have a particularly useful talent. I can take on the appearance of anyone I kill. I only needed to replace one man, of course."

"I don't believe you."

Arik said nothing, but placed his head in his hands. A moment later his body shape began to change. It became smaller, more human, and when he raised his head to look at her again, Amber gasped as she saw an ordinary-looking, middle-aged human man.

"He looked like this," Arik said, in a completely different voice, before he bowed his head again and returned to his former self. His eyes locked on Amber's. "A man who died because of yours and Joe's meddling."

"I'm sorry if our welcome seems a little... severe," Andrew continued as Amber stared in shocked

168

disbelief at Arik. "Maybe we should have laid on a party. After all, you *are* one of us."

Amber slowly turned her attention to him. She couldn't even be sure she had heard Andrew's words correctly. "One of... one of *you?* Why would you say that?"

"Because it's the truth. You always have been, just like your father- and your mother, come to that. You can't change your own nature. You can't suddenly become someone else, even though Arik *appeared* to do just that. People like to think they're masters of reinvention, but DNA has certain rules."

"How do you work that one out?" Amber retorted as she tried to ignore the deep unease that his words had stirred in her.

"I don't have days to go into all the tiny detail, so let me summarise. You had thought of the Order and the Lost as two separate entities, until your unexpected disappearance a year and a half ago. Then you learned the truth, didn't you? That we're really the same thing. We're heads and tails, left and right, up and down..." He grinned at her. "Do you know, I almost said *good and evil* then? But it's wrong-headed to think that way. The world isn't black and white. It's changed by instinct and opportunity."

"I already know that," Amber said stonily.

"I just said so, Amber. Did Daddy tell you before the pair of you disappeared? I'll bet he did."

Amber didn't say anything to that. It was painful to think of her dad and she couldn't help but be afraid for him. But Andrew was too interested in his own monologue to taunt her further on the matter.

"The names *Order* and *Lost* have been very convenient to us over the centuries," he continued. "What better way to control the destiny of the world and all its people than through the myth of two opposing groups? The idea has been fed to all our people for the last thousand years. Those who are brought up in or brought into either group believe that they're fighting for one side against the other. But the fact is, those of us who know the truth and have passed it carefully on for so long have a common goal."

"World domination?" Amber asked sarcastically. Her fear continued to ebb away. A deep anger burned inside her, and it lent courage. *If they're going to kill me, I'm not going to break down and cry,* she decided furiously.

"You're learning! For centuries we've worked towards the perfect conditions for humanity's meltdown. That's now finally been set in motion by the way. It's like a button being pressed very, very slowly. I suppose you've seen the news recently?"

"Yes, I've seen it."

"Such terrible things happening out there, don't you think? That's one of the reasons why this has become so *easy* for us, Amber. People never learn from the consequences of their mistakes. They just nurse their wounds for a while and then make the same mistakes again. Which is why *we* will... what's that biblical term? Inherit the earth."

Amber's head whirled with unanswered questions. "When Joe and I were in the Emptiness and you captured us, you said the Order was your enemy..."

"Well, it suited me to keep up the pretence before all our minions, didn't it? I couldn't very well tell you the truth." He tapped the side of his head with one spindly finger. "You're not *thinking*, Amber."

Andrew sat back in his seat. The harsh lighting made his eyes look almost like the sockets of a skull. "Whether they realise it or not, all of our people work towards the same goal. The time came for the fabric of the Order to fall apart. The official story is the end came about because of internal squabbles and the realisation that resistance is pointless. The Order has failed to prevent the end of the world. Anyone up to date with current affairs can see that much."

Andrew grinned at her. "Yes, the world in which you spent your childhood is finished, and we will rise from its ashes. And it's about time. Look at what humanity has done to itself, and to its planet."

"*You* did it," Amber accused him. "You caused all these wars and bombings and diseases and disasters and everything else."

"I'm afraid you overestimate us, my dear. Humanity would have done all these things regardless. All we had to do was stir everything up a little bit, give it a little direction, and make it... quicker. Bloodier. More certain."

"Why would you do all this?"

The man in the suit laughed and turned to Andrew. "She really is an idiot!"

"Naïve, certainly. But she'll be most useful to our cause, I assure you."

Andrew turned his attention back to Amber. "Why would we do all this? Because we become the new overlords of the world. We'll finally have a chance to step from the shadows and remake it in our own image. You recall the gateway that Joe took you through, some time ago?"

Amber nodded reluctantly. "I remember parts of what happened."

"Although he didn't know, Joe tested its strength and durability. We knew that Joe would find a way to point it somewhere on Earth and that the pathway would remain in place. Of course, he tried to change it as you passed through, so that the exit location wasn't quite what we expected." Andrew's amused smile had disappeared for the moment, replaced by a barely disguised, cold fury. "Many of us had to remain here in the Emptiness, once we realised that the pathway opened out into Antarctica. Hundreds had already stepped through, as Arik already told you."

Amber glared back at him. "Did most of them die in the cold? What a shame." She knew that she shouldn't make these people angry- they could do anything they wanted to her- but the words tumbled out of her mouth anyway.

"Yes. I thought so too, but we always learn from any setbacks we face." Andrew leaned back in his chair and looked thoughtfully at her. "It's time for humankind to be wiped out at long last- although I suppose we'll need to keep some of the creatures."

"Meat," Arik remarked. "You're an excellent source of protein. Some of you are, anyway."

Andrew laughed. "Arik is quite health-conscious."

"But *you're* human, or you were," Amber pointed out. "Aren't you?" she added uncertainly. *He's not,* she told herself at the same time. *Not inside. None of them are.*

"Ah. To be human." Andrew nodded as if he had expected Amber to say those words. "The fact is, Amber, that none of us with extraordinary powers are entirely human, whether we're in the Order or any other group or even if we think, as you appear to do, that we're free spirits. Oh, the majority have a mostly human ancestry. There are exceptions of course- those who have found us from other places." He glanced across at Arik with a smile. "But we have a separate lineage as well. A gift carried down generations which was given by those who crossed over from another world, over a thousand years ago."

"You're lying," Amber said automatically.

"No. I've nothing to gain from lying to you about your ancestry. It is what it is. They arrived unseen to begin with, they observed and they reproduced with the people of your world, and that's how it began. Their children and their descendants down the centuries all had special powers of one kind or another."

"That's ridiculous. How would aliens be able to reproduce with humans just like that?"

"You're *so* cynical, Amber. They weren't little green men with oversized heads. They came from a place very similar to our own world. In fact, you would recognise parts of it, had you seen it back then. You wouldn't be able to see it now, because the gateways that were linked to it have now long been destroyed, along with that world itself. It was much like the world you know, populated by people who were *more* than human. A different reality, where people had more potent abilities. Perhaps that helped eventually destroy their world- who knows. Anyway, I suppose you could call it a peaceful conquest, one that passed almost unnoticed. But things became complicated over time, as the secret of our existence was passed carefully on to our chosen next generation."

"So their world was like an alternative Earth where history had happened differently?"

"You could think of it that way. And some of the very first generation became the Sleepers." Andrew seemed to be enjoying his story far more than Amber enjoyed listening to it. "The Sleepers were the product of a quite fanciful idea. They were chosen to be kept asleep for many hundreds, perhaps thousands of years, after having firstly been given their instructions. They were to be awakened in the event of only the direst circumstances- the end of the world, something like that. And then they would save the world, to coin a well-worn cliché. At least, that's what the old stories say."

Sleepers. The word echoed through Amber's mind along with images of the great hall where the bodies in stasis were kept. *He doesn't know that they're here,* she thought in astonishment, and struggled to calm herself. *None of them know!*

"So it's just a story then?" she inquired finally.

Andrew shrugged. "Probably. They haven't made an appearance yet, and we'd know about it if they had. The end of the world is very nigh indeed. Of course, that leads to a rather stark choice for you to make. You can join us in our brave new world- or... well, how do I put this? We destroy *you*. I really do hope you'll choose option A, Amber. You're a bright girl with lots of potential. We could use someone like you."

"I thought the people of the Order were forbidden from having children," Amber said, deliberately trying not to think about his threat. "That's why my parents were thrown out, wasn't it? So how could these powers be passed down generations?"

"Oh, we're back to that are we? Of course those who know the truth are allowed to breed. How else do you think the abilities we have are passed on? DNA, Amber. Did you ever turn up for your biology lessons? As for your parents- well, they were unreliable. The Order became concerned that if they had any children, they wouldn't be able to ensure they kept the secrets about their identity when the time came. So they forbade them from starting a family. Of course, that didn't stop them, because you're here now, aren't you? The leadership have always monitored our more problematic people, particularly if they had children. Sometimes it's easier to observe and control people from a distance."

"So which is it to be?" Andrew asked as Amber mulled over everything he had told her. "There's only one sensible answer, if you bear in mind that the world is going to change regardless. It's a matter of whether you want to survive and be a part of it, or not."

Amber only half-listened to him. She found her attention drawn to the lights that hung down from the high ceiling. Somehow the flicker of those lights was being matched by a peculiar pulse inside her, not the pulse of her blood but of the strange force that was now a part of her. Perhaps her desperate situation had caused it to stir again.

But what can I do? I can't possibly defeat all of them!

In a moment the power inside her became a torrent of unstoppable force. The fibres of the ropes that bound her wrists and ankles unravelled from one another and fell as fine threads to the floor.

Amber wasn't at all sure what would happen to the illumination in the room, only that *something* would. It was the hottest object nearby, so she hoped it would be the easiest to affect. Part of her feared that the bulb would simply shatter and she would be plunged into total darkness surrounded by her enemies. But instead it flared with sudden, savage brilliance and lit up the entire room.

The intensity of the light didn't affect her- it made everything turn white yet she could still see it all in detail. But it had an unexpected, horrific effect on her captors. They screamed and stumbled backwards, clawing desperately at their faces. *It burns them,* Amber thought, although she had no idea what she had done to the light, other than amplify its effect many times over.

Run! a voice within urged her. *Run while you can!*

Even as she heard those frantic words, Amber saw Andrew's malevolent stare across the table. His companions continued to screech in pain and fear- even the monstrous Arik had retreated as far back as the nearest wall and hammered against it as if he frantically hoped to break through into some welcome darkness beyond.

But Andrew had quickly recovered his composure. Amber couldn't tell if she had somehow wounded him, but he looked as if he was trying to get up. The hatred in his eyes frightened her. It made them appear as little dark pools that swam in the surrounding light. *I am the void,* she imagined them whispering. *I am the absence of hope.*

Amber had no idea where to go, so she relied completely on instinct. She stood, turned and ran, and headed straight for a door near a distant corner. She feared that it would be locked, that she would pull helplessly at the handle until Andrew and then the others recaptured her.

But it opened and she ran heedlessly down the corridor beyond.

Doors keep opening for me, she thought numbly as she hurtled onwards.

What happens when they don't open anymore?

2

Andrew waited patiently for the light to subside and his companions to cease their idiotic panic.

"Alan," he said quietly. "We'll give her ten minutes. Then I need you to send a team after her. I want her found at *exactly* the right moment, do you understand? When she finds the *real* Sleepers. Do whatever it takes to ensure she can't wake them. Maybe one of your team can lead her away after you've hunted her down. I'm sure you can come up with some trick. And then I want the rest of you to destroy the pods and their contents. Melt them down and burn those creatures to oblivion."

Alan nodded. His skin had been burned red by Amber's assault, but Alan Michaels had never been one to show weakness or pain if he could help it. "Did you know she would do that?" he fumed.

"I suspected she might. It's clear that her powers have woken, otherwise she wouldn't be here at all." Andrew smiled. "Children are so predictable, aren't they? Your son performed his role admirably well. Which reminds me, where are Dean and Joe and Emma now?"

"I don't know at the moment," Alan said bluntly. "But I *do* know that they'll arrive in the maze sooner or later. They'll be drawn here. If Amber fails to find the Sleepers then they will."

"Then the same goes for them." Andrew glanced across at him. "The disguised portal worked then? The hole in the woods, or whatever it was that you engineered?"

For a moment Alan's smile returned. "Yes. Joe responded to the energy there, although he wouldn't have known it at the time. He would have caught a glimpse of... impossible things, shall we say. Very few others would have had such sensitivity to those special coordinates."

"Good. Then let's hope we can tame them all and make them see the error of their ways. They'll become immense tools in the right hands."

Andrew stood up and made his way over to the nearest wall. As he did, a faint glow surrounded him and lit up a portion of the wall when he pressed his hands against it. For a fleeting moment black veins appeared in his hands and over the surface of the wall itself. They moved like jagged, random cracks across the stonework as if Andrew had infected it.

"It's moving again," he said finally. "Other blocks this time, being shifted and rearranged. Their shapes and relationships change in so many different ways. It's an amazing piece of engineering, this place."

"Well, let's hope that one of these kids can master it," Alan said.

"Oh, one of them will. Perhaps they all will. That would be a bonus." Andrew removed his hands from the wall and listened carefully to the distant rumbling sound as parts of the vast maze moved slowly and reconfigured themselves. "No fortress exists that can't be breached one way or another, over time."

3

As before, when she had fled the hall of the Sleepers, Amber took a random path whenever she reached a junction. She reckoned that if *she* had no idea where she was going, her enemies might find it impossible to guess where she had fled.

But at the same time she feared that all she was doing was getting herself more and more lost.

If they capture me again then they'll just kill me, she warned herself. *I have to find a way out.*

Amber finally reached an empty room where she decided to rest a little longer. It was here as she sat in the half-lit gloom that Amber reflected on everything

Andrew had told her. Could they all be descended from the people of this alternative Earth? And had the Order really engineered the end of the world?

It might all be true. Amber remembered the things her dad had said that night when they left their home sixteen months ago. In a way it all sounded similar. *Everywhere we went I looked around me and I saw so much hate, even back then,* she remembered. *The news became more and more flooded with stories of stabbings and shootings, people trying to kill as many other people as possible. It just became ordinary after a while.*

And yet everything about this was too difficult to believe unless she decided to believe everything. *Maybe I'm too scared of the truth,* she thought, and shivered.

Everything felt hopeless. Whatever the truth might be, none of the things that were going on in the world could be stopped. The Order had already seen to that. They would be the new lords of whatever remained once the bloodbath was finally over.

What can I do? she wondered desperately. *I can't hide here forever. I need to find a way back, but what will I have to go back to? I need to find Dad. Maybe he can do something, maybe not, but either way I just want to be with him, even if the end of the world is coming.*

Especially if the end of the world is coming.

Amber recalled how a few years ago she had desperately wanted to be different to everyone else, to stand out from the crowd. Then, when her life had changed that summer a year and a half ago, she had discovered the truth- that she *was* different, only in a way that no one else could understand except her dad, Joe and Emma.

She didn't want to be different anymore. Not like this. But even if she found her way back and found her dad, a normal life would never be possible.

I've seen what's going on in the world and I can't ignore the things I now know, she told herself. *Everyone else just walks around as if they're sleepwalking into oblivion.*

Sleepwalking, Amber thought, and suddenly realised what it was that she had to do.

She had to find her way back to the hall of the Sleepers and once there, work out a way to wake them up and release them from their centuries-old prisons.

Amber thought about it a little longer and then shook her head miserably. The idea was ridiculous. How could she possibly find her way back? This maze of corridors and rooms might go on for many miles, and she was already lost- in fact she had made herself as lost as possible in her panic. She could wander for days and still never find the Sleepers again. Even if by some miracle she *did* discover them, what then?

"Nothing," Amber whispered.

She wondered how she might communicate with the Sleepers. Through their dreams perhaps? After all, they were asleep. Maybe that would change their brain patterns and wake them up so that *they* could free themselves.

Then an unpleasant possibility occurred to her.

Had she imagined the voice that she had heard in the hall?

4

Amber walked until she reached a corridor that looked murkier and dirtier than the others. Patches of mould infested the walls, floor and ceiling. The damp smell reminded Amber of some of the places she and her dad had lived in. Some of the doors along its length lay partly open, and beyond them she saw scenes of desolation- rooms crammed with piles of paper, cobwebs and dust, other rooms that contained rotting furniture and seeped with dampness that rippled through ancient wallpaper. Amber didn't stop for long enough to investigate thoroughly, but they all looked oddly normal, like abandoned offices from the world she knew.

She walked swiftly to where the passageway came to an end and a flight of stairs descended into the gloom. She saw some lights flicker on and off but they barely cut through the darkness.

This can't be the right way, she thought desperately. *I would have remembered this.* But when she glanced back the corridor looked in even worse condition. A thick, black infestation of mould covered the walls, along with something else that looked like bunches of long black fingers that extended down from the ceiling and sprouted from the dismal walls. It definitely hadn't looked that bad a moment ago.

Just like Patrick's cottage, Amber thought fearfully.

Then one of the doors opened a little further with a faint creak. Amber froze to the spot as a familiar figure emerged from the room beyond.

It was the creature that had once appeared as an old woman, but it looked different now - desperate and frightened. As Amber stared, it fell to its knees and fixed her with a pleading look. "Don't hurt me," it begged, and Amber couldn't suppress the shudder that went through her as she looked into its dirty yellow-brown eyes for a moment.

She steeled herself against feeling sorry for it. "I should have killed you. I still can."

"Oh, I know, I know, and you probably should after everything I've done and how I've tried to trick you, but please hear me out, Amber. Please listen to me, that's all. What harm can it do?"

All the harm in the world, Amber thought. *That's one of the reasons why everything is the way it is. People listen to the wrong voices.*

"No," she said, aware of how close she had walked to the top of the stairs. She took a step towards the creature and it crept back several paces, then lifted up a bony hand as if it expected her to burn it to ashes. "You're just trying trick me again," Amber continued.

"No, I promise you that I'm not! I want to give you the truth."

"And what is the truth? That I'm just like all of you and I should join with you? I've already heard that. Andrew told me the full story."

It whimpered at the sound of that name. "Andrew never gives anyone the *whole story*," it hissed then, suddenly angry. "I should have been a member of the inner circle. Not him. He's never fully renounced his humanity." It stepped carefully towards her until Amber raised a hand to warn it once again.

"I'm going," Amber said, "and if you try to follow me I'll destroy you. I'll do it slowly."

"Stay with me," it croaked. Amber thought for a moment that its appearance had begun to change once again, to become almost human. She heard a faint popping, cracking sound, as if the monster's bones moved around and adjusted themselves. "We can leave this place, you and I. The Emptiness is vast. I know places here where even *they* won't look. I just want to keep you safe."

Amber laughed at that. The idea was ridiculous, but then after a moment it also sounded as if it might be true.

"We could be together, you and I. Why, you..." Now its voice had become exactly like that of a kindly old lady again. "You could be my little granddaughter!"

Amber suddenly realised that the creature stood right next to her. It reached out a thin, wrinkled finger to touch her cheek. Amber grabbed swiftly at it but too late. The touch burned worse than anything she could have imagined, and Amber howled in agony.

She seized the creature's bony wrist, and the forces inside her leapt in defence. As the light poured from her, then down its arm and over its body, its eyes widened in fear. The creature's mouth opened to scream but no sound emerged.

"*I said I'd destroy you,*" Amber heard herself say as she finally let go of her enemy and it fell to the floor. It writhed for a moment and then lay still. When the

186

light faded nothing remained of the creature except a faint black husk of char. She had burned it inside and out.

Amber looked away, faint and light-headed for a moment. After a short while she headed on down the steps and kept one hand on the side wall to try to steady herself, but she had no need to. She no longer trembled.

For the first time in a long while, Amber didn't feel afraid.

5

Sometime later, Amber emerged from a low, dimly-lit tunnel into a gloomy hall which looked like an older, darker version of the one with the Sleepers. Just as in the other hall, pods were embedded in the walls. But almost all the lights inside and near to them were either switched off or no longer worked. A few flickered and made faint buzzing noises.

She stepped further into the hall and peered at the occupants of the pods. Then she recoiled in disgust. The bodies inside had almost completely wasted away. Most of them were little more than skeletons or mummified remains.

Was this another generation of Sleepers? Amber thought as she tried to overcome her revulsion. *An older group from further back in time? Did they rot away because their equipment failed and they couldn't survive the long sleep through the centuries?*

Were they conscious when that happened?

But then, to her shock a voice spoke up. It sounded like nothing more than a faint whisper in her head.

Help us, it begged.

Amber stared wildly around the grim hall and wondered if she had finally lost her mind. None of these Sleepers could possibly still be alive. She must have imagined the voice.

You must release us, the voice pleaded. *If we remain imprisoned, the renegades will control all the free worlds that still exist. They will rule unchallenged. Their cruelty will be total and eternal.*

Those ominous words filled Amber with fear. "But..." Tentatively she walked nearer to one of the pods and looked up at the wasted remains inside with a mixture of unease and disgust. "You're dead," she said finally. "You're all dead. Apart from... but I don't know how to find..."

Those Sleepers elsewhere in the maze, who looked as if they were still alive? Amber thought the voice sounded almost amused. *They are part of a complex illusion. They are not real- not in a way you could understand, anyway.*

"Not real?" Amber shook her head in disbelief. "But I... I saw them breathing... they hadn't decayed..."

When we were put into the deep sleep we knew that sooner or later the descendants of our people would become corrupt, that they would seek to destroy us if they could, fearful of what might happen to them should we wake. Those who placed us here knew the same. And so the illusions were created, and the knowledge of them kept safe- so that in the very remote likelihood that someone managed to access the centre of the maze, they would probably encounter one of them - not the true Sleepers.

"How many of these illusions are there?"

Two thousand, one hundred and fifty-three.

"Two thousand..." Amber almost laughed. Maybe the maze was far larger than even she had thought.

Some of the Sleepers within these rooms appear to be alive and asleep, whereas others look as we do, long dead and decayed. But they are all illusions, no matter their state. We are the only true Sleepers. The twelve of us in this hall.

"But..." Amber turned to look at the wasted remains in each of the pods. "You're all long dead..."

An illusion hangs over this place also, Amber. Don't believe all the things you see.

Amber shivered. "I don't know what to believe. That's all I know right now."

It may be that the time of our discovery draws near. You had the misfortune to encounter some of the creatures that were once our people. They have spent decades, perhaps even centuries, looking for us throughout the Emptiness. They are closer now than ever before, even though this place is infused with great science beyond your understanding, weaved into it from the beginning. I suppose you could call it a powerful magic.

"Magic or science?" Amber asked. "It can't be both."

Can it not? How do you think you're able to understand what I'm saying? A thousand years separate our languages, but we had a way to overcome such problems even then.

Amber took a sharp intake of breath. She hadn't thought about that.

The Sleeper continued, *You've seen how this whole area is built like a maze. But the maze moves periodically. You could think of it as a vast array of interlocking pieces, a sort of three-dimensional jigsaw, although the reality is more fluid than that. So complex, in fact, that we could only be found by someone who was meant to find us, who could move all the pieces in the right way at the same time. Tell me, have you noticed how easily you've opened doors here?*

"So I was meant to find you?" Amber nodded slowly. It made sense. "But how did you know I was here?"

We sensed you from some distance away. In fact we sensed you when you burst into the Emptiness, for the first time and then again only a short while ago. The power you used was considerable and sent ripples across this world.

"I didn't really know what I was doing," Amber admitted.

Such is the way of our talents, at first. Wisdom comes only with age. long after raw power.

"I guess."

Although we sleep, we remain aware. But that awareness is without real power or influence. We touch the worlds in brief and subtle ways, nothing more than that. Still, that's why we were put to sleep- so that only the direst circumstances would wake us. I assume that your world is on the brink, or else you would not have found this place.

"On the brink?"

Of destroying itself- or more correctly, being destroyed by those who occupy it.

"Yes. It's been that way for a while but it suddenly got even worse in the last few months. I know that the Order have worked to make it happen faster. I suppose that's why some of them hid here and waited for the end so they could step out and rule."

That way be one of their plans. But although they eagerly await the destruction of your world by its people, they have also drawn ever closer to this exact place, these dimensions within the Emptiness where we sleep. This hidden place.

"Andrew said you were just a story," Amber recalled.

Soft laughter filled her head, neither amused nor pleasant. *They found you as you wandered the maze. We could do nothing about that. Allow me to guess what happened. They interviewed you, in a manner of speaking, in one of the outer rooms. This Andrew is, I suspect, one of the current leadership...*

"I think so, yes."

...and he happened to casually mention us, knowing all the while that you were being unknowingly led towards our location.

"You mean *he* knew that *I* knew about them?! How?"

Perhaps he simply guessed. Maybe he worked out that you could lead them to us one way or another.

Either way, I can assure you that he knows we exist, if he ranks highly amongst the Order.

Amber said nothing. She had been tricked. Had she unwittingly left a trail that would lead her enemies here, to the Sleepers?

I have more to tell you. There came a point when we used what little power we had left to send a message. You will already know of the Guardians, mystical and powerful members of the Order.

"I do," Amber murmured.

Guardians are appointed very infrequently and for no reason that anyone within the Order can fathom. A member of the Order may become a Guardian without any warning, suddenly been given a specific task along with the great powers required to carry it out.

No matter what questions are asked of them by other members of the Order, the Guardians never reveal how these persuasions were given to them - they can't, because they have no knowledge of us. We touch their minds in a dream, and when they wake they know only what they must do. In this way we have managed to repress the worst excesses of the Order in the last hundred years or so, when they have been responsible for more wars and atrocities than ever before. We, the Sleepers, create these Guardians. We have always done so, whenever we can, and no one has known that they are our doing.

Amber nodded, dumbfounded. She tried to imagine what the world might have been like without those interventions by the Sleepers. Even worse, apparently.

Our capacity to create Guardians has weakened over the centuries. We created one final one, in the knowledge that we could never repeat the process again. Our power to do so had simply withered away.

"That was the one you sent to Joe."

Indeed it was. You could call it our last desperate gamble. The Guardian attempted to reveal the truth about us to Joe, without knowing that it was indeed the Sleepers he referred to. But already the power that we instilled in him had weakened. Joe remembered fragments, perhaps, but nothing more. Still, the encounter with the Guardian awakened his powers, and somehow the Order found out about this. Suspecting that some interference had happened when the Guardian met the two of you, they closed in, but you escaped them.

"They found us anyway, in the Emptiness," Amber recalled.

The leadership of the Order have controlled much of the Emptiness for a long time, although many of its secrets remain a mystery to them. It was inevitable, perhaps, that they would capture you. And when they learned that Joe had the ability to open doorways between your world and the Emptiness, they decided to test his ability in more detail.

"The gateway," Amber said bitterly. "It was all a trick."

A trick? Perhaps. A test, certainly. Although we could do nothing to help, we were aware of what happened. Somehow he managed to bend that gateway to his will, and transport you back to your world.

"My dad and Joe's aunt became more worried about the Order after that," Amber recalled. "Then they decided we all had to disappear and never meet again. That happened *really* suddenly."

At the time, it would have been the only available course of action. Had you remained where you were, I'm sure all four of you would have been tortured until the truth poured out as you begged for the pain to stop.

"I don't know how we managed to avoid them for so long. But we did, until they came to our apartment. They found us in the end."

"Amber!"

She whirled around to see her dad standing in one of the doorways that led from the hall. Dumbfounded, she stood and stared for a moment and then tried to run towards him, but her legs wouldn't move.

He walked across the hall towards her, and as if his movement broke a spell Amber rushed into his embrace and they held each other tightly for a long while.

"How did you find me?" she murmured. "I've been lost here for... I don't know how long..."

"I was lost too." His hand reached out and stroked her hair. *He hasn't done that for years,* Amber thought. *Not since I was ten probably.*

"I woke up here in this maze," he continued. "I sensed that you were nearby."

"You woke up *here?*" Amber felt puzzled. It didn't seem right.

"We need to get out," he continued. "They're hunting for you."

"You know about that? I mean, yes we have to... no, wait!" Amber took a deep breath and tried to calm herself. "There's something I need to tell you about the Sleepers..."

"The Sleepers?"

Amber did her best to explain. Finally she added, "The other ones, those that look as if they're still alive and just sleeping, well they're *not* the real ones, and there are others as well, all around this maze, but the only *real* Sleepers are these ones, and..." She shook her head in frustration. "I have to wake them!"

"So these are the *real* Sleepers? You're certain?"

"I'm totally certain."

He nodded. "In that case, we have to get away."

Amber blinked. "What do you mean? If we don't wake them then the Order will control everything! Don't you understand?! The Sleepers knew that one day the Order would become corrupt and destroy the people they were supposed to protect!"

He held her shoulders and looked intently at her. "Amber, the Sleepers are all dead. The technology that kept them alive failed centuries ago. Look around and see for yourself."

"No!" She turned to look at them. "Speak to him!" she pleaded. "Tell him everything you told me."

But the Sleeper's whispering voice did not come to her. Her dad gave her an odd look and then gazed around at the decayed bodies in their partly broken pods. Amber could tell from the look in his eyes that he had heard nothing.

"You have to believe me," she pleaded. "One of them spoke to me. They said all sorts of things, about the Guardians and how *they* were the ones to create them, how they sent the Guardian to Joe but it didn't quite work as planned because they'd lost almost all their power... and the one who spoke to me said *I* could release them."

"It would mean the end of our world, if you woke them."

"If the Order take control of everything, then *that* will mean the end of the world as we know it," Amber retorted. "Do you want us to be their slaves? That's if they even allowed us to survive. I don't think they would, unless we agreed to become servants to their cause."

Her dad didn't say anything, and in the silence that followed Amber felt an unpleasant thought occur to her. "Wait a minute," she said softly. "Andrew mentioned the Sleepers and I think that was so I would do something to escape and run. Because the maze was always going to pull me towards the them. That's what it's for. When the right person is found it changes shape and the corridors lead them to the chamber. To this place. It's the perfect defence. Andrew and the other leaders of the Order were able to find the outer reaches of the maze but they could never get further in. And yet *you* were able to find it. You said you even woke up here. How is that possible?"

"We can talk about all this later, Amber. But we have to get out of here and back to our world. I think I know a way. Then we can go back to our lives..."

Amber shook her head stubbornly. "There's nothing to go back to!"

He looked intently at her. "Amber, you know I love you more than anything. I need you to just do this one thing for me. For the world."

She looked into his eyes and suddenly a cold feeling washed over her. She couldn't move. She could barely breathe. A mad, frantic thought hurtled through her mind.

They're not his eyes. They look the same, but they're someone else's eyes looking out of his face. How couldn't I see that before?! There's no love there at all.

"Amber, what's the matter?" He reached for her again but she took a couple of hurried steps backwards. "Don't touch me!" she warned.

A faint smile creased his lips for a moment. "Amber, you need to calm down."

"You're not him," she said bluntly. "You're not my dad."

"Amber, you're not making any sense. First you start babbling nonsense about these dead and rotting Sleepers and how they somehow spoke to you, and now you tell me that I'm not even me. Does that sound sane to you?"

She couldn't think of anything to say, and he continued, "I didn't want to say this, Amber, but I've been worried about you for a while. Your behaviour has been... what's the best word for it? Erratic. Disturbed, sometimes."

"Disturbed." Her voice trembled. "I'm not... I'm not disturbed. I'm not imagining things."

In a moment he stood next to her again, and he had put his arms around her. She tried to wriggle free but couldn't. "It's all right," he whispered. "I'll take you back. Everything will be fine..."

"No!" Amber shrieked, and her strength returned, so suddenly that she couldn't control herself. She grabbed his shoulders and pushed him back with such force that he flew back about ten yards.

"Show yourself," she hissed when he sat up, a cunning smile on his face. "Show your true face!"

Whether or not she had forced it to, Amber couldn't tell, but slowly the creature that had pretended to be her father revealed itself. Thin and haggard-looking, its skin became drawn back over bones that could not be human. Its eyes became smaller and darker, its fingers longer.

It rushed at her on all fours, claw-like fingers scrabbling against the stone floor as dark energy crackled over its misshapen body. Amber's powers slammed against it, and the creature howled in agony and frustration, held in place. Amber concentrated all her fury and the hatred she felt on her enemy, and finally it burned away to nothing more than a faint scar on the stone floor.

Amber felt entirely empty as she sagged to her knees and stared at the space which her enemy had occupied only moments before. *It fooled me,* she thought numbly. *At least it would have done if it hadn't mentioned waking up here. Somehow I didn't think that was right. What would have happened if I'd let it take me away from here? I'd have been killed and the rest of the Order would have been led to the Sleepers.*

Did they intend for me to lead them to this place? Is that what I've done anyway?

She heard footsteps and saw six others approach one of the doorways. But no sooner had she seen them than the doorway itself vanished. For a moment she heard a dull grinding noise, and howls of frustration that faded away. *It's the maze,* Amber thought. *The maze is moving again. Did I do that?*

She couldn't feel any movement, and yet she sensed it in another way. A picture came to her of a three-dimensional map of the complex structure, and she immediately saw the tiny part of it that had just moved, as if its colour was different to the rest of the map.

When the image in her head faded, Amber saw that one of the doorways had changed. It looked darker than it had before, and she couldn't see any part of the passageway beyond. Then she heard footsteps approach and her heart sank. *More of them,* she thought in despair.

Then three figures appeared out of the darkness, and Amber could scarcely believe her eyes.

"Joe," she whispered, but even when he ran to her and looked into her eyes, Amber still couldn't fully believe. Too much had happened. She smiled weakly, swept up in a dream. "Is it really you?" she whispered.

THE WAKING

Time passed in a blur. Amber remembered afterwards that she had hugged Joe so tightly and cried so much that she thought she wouldn't be able to stop. They breathlessly exchanged their stories almost without pause and even talked over each other from time to time.

Afterwards Joe introduced her to Dean, who he said had helped save them just before they managed to reach the Emptiness.

"How did you get here?" she asked Joe.

"I knew you were somewhere here. When we stepped through the light and down the stairs... something moved. Part of this place, I think."

Amber smiled. "Yes. It did. And I think it may have saved me."

Joe looked around the pods. "What are all these dead bodies doing here?"

"They're not dead," Amber said. "These are the Sleepers. I spoke with one of them."

She watched Joe's expression change. As he looked at the others Amber realised that they too had heard of them. "These are the real ones," she continued. "There are others around this place but they're fakes, put here to distract anyone from the Order who might somehow find their way into the middle of the maze and try to destroy them." Amber looked nervously around. "They're closing in. They know I've found them. We need to..."

"...wake them," Joe said immediately, "and we haven't got much time."

"The Sleepers were put in place to guard against their own people- future generations of the Order who had turned against the values of the Order," Emma spoke up. "It could be that their mission is to destroy those people, once they're awakened and released. But what happens after that?"

Joe shrugged warily. "I don't know. What?"

"*We* are also people of the Order. Can we be sure that they won't kill us too? Who knows, maybe they'll even kill themselves once this is done, to make sure the Order is gone forever. So that the whole cycle can never be repeated."

"Maybe we're to be trusted to make sure it never happens again," Amber suggested.

Emma shook her head. "They have no reason to trust us. Human nature is what it is. They wouldn't go to such lengths to protect themselves and then allow certain people of the Order to live."

Joe looked to Amber. "What do you think?"

"I don't know," Amber said. " But if we stand here and do nothing, the Order will come for us, and there'll be so many of them that we'll stand no chance. They won't make any mistake this time. If we *can* wake the Sleepers then maybe we stand a chance. This might be the only way to destroy the Order. Going back to a world that they have absolute control over isn't an option, is it?"

"I'm not going back," Dean said quietly. "Not until they're all dead. Every single one."

"You said you spoke with one of the Sleepers," Dean said to Amber. "Can you try doing that again?"

Amber turned to address the Sleeper who had communicated with her before, but before she could speak the woman's voice came again, harsh and urgent. This time all four of them heard it.

Every minute you spend here is a far longer time in your own world, where with every passing day thousands and eventually millions will die in wars, atrocities and disasters, caused in part by the Order. We can swiftly locate those responsible, including those amongst them who are searching through the maze at this moment, and destroy them. We can find those others who do the work of the Order and ensure that they too are exterminated. Even now it will be too late to halt much of their evil, but something of your world may yet be saved.

The companions looked in sober silence at one another.

A moment later Joe, Amber and Dean had linked hands, although none of them knew who had moved first. It was as if they blinked and a moment later they had made the decision to wake and release the Sleepers, even though none of them could say *how* they were going to do so. Emma watched in wonderment and shielded her eyes as a stream of pulsing light spread between the three children and then all around the hall.

It's as if we're the ones who are sleeping, Amber thought as the powers of her companions flooded through her. *We're still in a dream, but we're about to wake. And we've no idea what reality we'll wake up into.*

A vast tremor went through the whole hall and the light dimmed. A huge groan sounded as if the earth itself had begun to shift or an impossibly huge creature stirred deep within the fabric of the world.

Joe felt the miraculous energy pour from him, through Amber and Dean and then back into him like a continuous river, just as theirs coursed through him, a river shared by the three of them. An intense feeling of bliss and wonder overcame him, but it was tinged with fear. He sensed shadows that flickered nearby, as if he, Amber and Dean were trapped on an island made of light and a sea of utter blackness, a cold void, separated them from everything else.

A memory blossomed in Joe's mind. It wasn't his, but it came from the brief time he had spent with the Guardian a year and a half ago. He felt as if he stepped through an unstoppable vision.

I know how to do this, he thought in bewilderment. *I know how to release them. I don't know how the Guardian knew. Maybe the Sleepers told him somehow, and he passed it to me. How else could he or anyone else know about working these things? They're from so many centuries ago. This machinery was set up to protect them until the right people came here. It's already reacting to us.*

The ancient pods began to glow even as the other illumination in the hall continued to fade. A faint hum buzzed through all the pieces of machinery. Dust and dirt fell to the floor as wires and cables vibrated. Another enormous groan and rumble shuddered through the walls.

He heard Amber's voice inside his head, her words full of joyous disbelief. *It's working! It's really working!*

Not yet, he replied, as the noise became steadily louder and vibrated through his head.

Then he heard Dean's voice, faint but panic-stricken. *We're going to lose ourselves! We'll become just like them!*

Not if we're strong, Amber replied, but Joe thought she sounded uneasy too.

Sudden bright white light flared from the edges of the pods, and the companions saw an astonishing change happen. Flesh began to appear on the skeletal remains inside the pods, and gradually the wasted figures became the bodies of men and women. Eventually, with the miraculous process complete, the light around the pods faded away. Joe, Dean and Amber let go of one another and the light that surrounded them also disappeared. Then they flinched in fear as the glass doors of the pods abruptly shattered.

Amber slowly approached one of the pods, which held a woman with long dark hair and blue eyes. She looked no older than about thirty but must have been alive for many hundreds of years, hidden behind the powerful illusion of this place. "Did you speak to me?" she murmured, but the woman only stared at her.

Amber shuddered as she wondered what it might have been like to wait that long. Would she have slept throughout those long centuries? Would she have dreamed? What would someone's dreams be like if they slept for such a long period of time?

For better or worse it's done now, she thought as the Sleepers all stepped out of their pods at the same time. A faint glow surrounded each one of them. By now it was the only light left in the hall.

The young woman with the dark hair stepped forward and looked at them. The intensity in her eyes was unsettling. Amber detected a faint, musty odour, and for a moment she saw something that rippled under the woman's skin. She took a step back. "What... are you?" she whispered.

But the woman only smiled faintly at her, and then looked further away into the gloom of the hall.

Have we done the right thing? Amber asked herself, and wondered if her companions had the same misgivings. But at the same time she felt as if an immense weight had been lifted from her shoulders.

The woman turned and headed towards one of the exits, and the other Sleepers followed her. None gave the companions so much as a passing glance. They stared resolutely ahead, their thoughts perhaps already full of the tasks they would now carry out. Amber shivered. Although outwardly human, they somehow moved like machines, focused only on their tasks, with no need or desire for anything beyond them.

Progress will kill everyone, she thought suddenly, and turned away.

"Something's happening over there," Dean said quietly after the companions stood in stunned silence for a long while. His hand shook as he pointed across the hallway to one of the exits, which now opened out into what looked like empty space. When the companions stepped a little nearer they saw faint, indistinct points of light.

Stars, Amber thought, astonished. *That isn't a doorway at all- not a normal one anyway. Is it the way back?*

But then some unpleasant possibilities occurred to her. What if this gateway was nothing of the sort? What if it led to some hellish place instead of Earth? Or simply left them trapped somewhere for all eternity?

The gateway slowly changed so that the edges where it met the corridor rippled and gave the portal an almost fluid look. More stars appeared in the portion of space they could see. Occasionally the companions felt a light breeze that blew from one direction and then another.

"Is that the way back?" Amber asked.

Joe said quietly, "No. But I know where it goes. Back to the centre. The safe place."

"Safe place?" Amber stared at him.

"The only one that's left." Joe reached out and squeezed her hand. "You'll remember when we get there."

FURTHER IN AND FASTER

When the companions stepped through the portal they felt smooth ground under their feet, although they saw nothing of their surroundings. They made their way slowly forward until after a while the ground became softer and more uneven. Faint light from somewhere unknown began to filter through to the passageway, which opened out gradually into a wider area. As the level of light gradually increased they could see that their environment had begun to change in other ways too. Faint large shapes nearby revealed themselves to be trees. A light breeze sighed faintly through the vastness of the forest. Leaves rustled and unimaginable creatures scuttled through the blackness of the undergrowth.

As the companions walked they saw points of starlight in the gaps between the trees. Soon the light provided by the stars became so strong that they no longer needed to hold onto one another, and they walked more quickly along the path as it widened further.

Although none of them said so, the place through which they walked had become much more than a woodland. With the strengthening of the light they saw that the path appeared like a tunnel of green-hued brilliance, pierced by celestial light but warm and comforting.

To Amber it felt like walking up the garden path to a home she had never had but had always imagined- a beautiful country cottage where she and her dad could live safely and in peace. Even as the beauty of the forest took her breath away she felt a desperate grief take hold of her⸗ a stone inside that would drag her down and drown her in sorrow if she allowed it.

He would want me to be strong, she reminded herself, but even as she tried to be strong the tears came anyway. *I thought it was him at first. I really thought it was him!*

But then, as they pressed on further into the forest Amber felt his faint presence, and it grew steadily with each turn of the path they followed. One part of her felt a quiet excitement stir, a certainty that he was somewhere here and that she would see him soon. Her other, angry and cynical side silently tried to quash that hope, insistent that this would simply turn out to be another trick of the Order.

But the peculiar optimism won out. It grew and blossomed into a riot of deep love that had always been a part of her but which she had never fully expressed. Tears of relief rolled down Amber's cheeks as she hurried along. It was all she could do not to scream her joy around the shadowy forest and up into the luminescent sky.

Joe's thoughts were more complex and troubled. He wondered what form the justice of the Sleepers would take. Would they locate all the remaining members of the Order and destroy them? Or was it already too late? *Did we do the right thing?* he asked himself, but the question could not be answered, or perhaps had too many answers.

Dean walked a little behind the others, astonished at the transformation of the woodland into a hall of light and power. He felt almost as if he could fly and soar through the forest, consumed by the sheer energy of this place.

He wondered what would happen to his parents when the Sleepers caught them, which he had no doubt they would. *I hate them both so much,* he thought, but immediately afterwards he wondered if things could ever have been different. Did he hate them enough to want them to suffer and die at the hands of the Sleepers?

But then he reminded himself of all the things they had done. Pictures loomed in his mind, of his father's casual violence, utter contempt for humanity and mocking smile- and his mother's cold indifference to everything about him. She had never felt anything for him other than disgust.

They almost destroyed me, Dean thought savagely. *They deserve everything they get. They were monsters.*

Does that mean that one day, I might be?

As before, Joe found that the further into the woodland they walked, the more quickly they appeared to cover the ground. He had expected this to happen. *The cottage is always there at the centre,* he reminded himself. *It's eternal, and everything else spins around it. Maybe whole worlds.*

When they finally turned a corner and saw the cottage before them, bathed in the light of a million stars and alive with rippling power, the companions stopped for a moment. Mysterious forces swirled around and buffeted them one way and then the other. "There'll be a storm," Joe spoke up. "A storm that reaches through every world. The Sleepers are just a small part of it. This is the only place where we can be safe."

"I think I saw someone in there, for a moment," Dean said. "Did anyone else?"

The others stared when Amber strode ahead down the path to the door. "What are you doing?" Emma called out, but Amber didn't stop or glance back. After a moment she broke into a run, and when the door opened and a figure stood on the threshold, nothing more than a silhouette against the warm illumination inside, Amber threw herself forward to be caught in its embrace.

FIVE YEARS LATER

I've forgotten so much now, but I remember one thing more than anything else.

The absolute, perfect silence when we stepped back into the world will stay with me forever. Sometimes, even now, I find it difficult to deal with. We grew up in a world which was noisy, switched-on and so full of people rushing around and things going on that the new reality was difficult to adjust to.

I'll look up into the sky and wish, just for a moment, that I can hear the faint whine of an aeroplane passing by, glittering in the sun, maybe taking people on holiday somewhere.

If we cross a railway line I'll imagine a train rattling past full of people on their way to or from work, or on their way to visit friends or family.

We'll pass through towns sometimes and pause to look at the empty, silent buildings, open and abandoned, imagining the noise and bustle of people going in and out.

But I don't miss the screaming intensity of a world crammed full of people arguing, fighting, competing for attention, always trying to get ahead of one another and trample on one another. All their spiteful effort counted for nothing in the end.

The simple things stand out as we travel through this quiet world. The changing of the seasons. The stillness of the city streets. The wild beauty of the abandoned meadows and woods. The sighing of the wind and the shapes of the clouds. And then comes the night, when the galaxy opens out above us.

No matter the destruction, the old world had to end.

We found that much of the world we knew had already changed beyond anything we could have imagined. Wars, disease, famine, natural disasters had all happened around the same time. Catastrophe heaped on catastrophe. The Order ended the old way of things, but they didn't survive to see the fruits of their labour.

We've found no one else. What will we do if we ever meet others? I'm not sure. I'm not even certain that I want to see other people. But why were we allowed to survive? None of us can answer that question. Amber asked me days ago, "Why are we still here?" She's still searching for a reason. Emma, Luke and Dean have all asked the same question. We've spent long nights discussing it, but our theories count for nothing. I think we just find comfort in talking, in hearing one another's voices.

Wherever we go, I feel like an explorer from another world. That's how alien everything is now. The lights of civilisation have gone out, but in their place we now see so many stars. At night, it's almost like being back in the Emptiness- and in many ways, that's exactly what our environment has become. An empty but beautiful expanse waiting to be explored. Nature has begun to reclaim the concrete of human activity.

One day, when the beauty of this new world has become ordinary to me, I'll write my story. I guess it started in a classroom all those years ago, when I thought I saw something made by dust in the sunlight. I feared for a while that I might be losing my mind, but instead the world around me went mad. It was a horror too great to last, and maybe that's the most hopeful way to think about it. No matter how terrible things become, nothing lasts forever.

And that alone gives us hope, as we walk the silent world.

Thank you for reading this book. I hope you enjoyed it. If so, please do take the time to leave a review on Amazon or Goodreads. Authors depend on reviews for other readers to discover their work. Thanks!

Simon Williams